Is it over between Ginger and Ben?

"Guess what, Ginger?" Ben cried. "They put me in at wide receiver."

"Tell her the rest," Todd said, turning to me. "He scored the winning touchdown! We won the tournament because of him! And now the guys are throwing a party in Ben's honor."

"So?" I asked.

"You have to come," Todd said. "The guys will expect Ben to bring a date."

I could feel the anger boiling up inside me.

"You guys make me sick," I snapped. "Last week you sneaked around behind my back so you could go to a party with a bunch of dumb cheerleaders, and now suddenly you've decided that you want me around again, because Mr. Studly Wide Receiver needs a girl gazing at him adoringly to boost his image. Well, thanks, but no thanks. I'm not a book you can take off the shelf when it's convenient for you and put back when it's not. And you know what?" I paused dramatically. "I don't even need you anymore, Ben Campbell. I have Scott Masters waiting for me outside—you know him, the famous senior? He wouldn't sneak around behind my back to spend an evening with a bunch of cheerleaders!"

See back of book for details.

Ginger's New Crush

#5

Ginger's New Crush

Janet Quin-Harkin

Troll Associates

Published by Troll Associates, Inc. Rainbow Bridge is a trademark of Troll Associates.

Produced by Daniel Weiss Associates, Inc.
33 West 17th Street
New York, New York 10011

Printed in the United States of America.

10 9 8 7 6 5 4 3 2 1

To Audrey Costello, in appreciation of her friendship, her hiking stamina, and her great critiquing skills.

1

We scrambled up the rocky path toward the top of Spirit Rock, the sweat running into our eyes and plastering our hair to our foreheads. It was late Sunday afternoon. I had been studying all day for a big English test with my best friends, Roni, Karen, and Justine. About four o'clock, I decided that I couldn't stand being cooped up in the house any longer. I told my friends I had something special to show them.

"How much farther, Ginger?" Karen gasped.

"Not much farther now," I said. "When we come around the corner, we'll be at the summit."

"I hope it'll be worth it." Karen wiped her hair out of her eyes with a dusty hand, leaving brown streaks across her face.

"It will, trust me," I said.

Roni looked around. "Where's Justine?" she asked.

We exchanged a worried glance. "She can't have gotten lost again," I said. "She was with us a second ago."

"Justine!" we yelled, our voices bouncing off the craggy rocks.

"Wait up, you guys. Don't leave me!" Justine's voice echoed from below us. "You're going too fast."

I gave Roni and Karen an exasperated grin. We'd already had to stop at least ten times because Justine got a rock in her shoe, Justine's hair was coming down, Justine was being chased by a bee, or Justine's shoes were getting dirty.

"Come on, Justine. Only a few more yards," I called encouragingly. "We have to make it to the top in time for the sunset. That's the whole point."

Justine's face came into sight around the corner. Usually her makeup was perfect and her blond ponytail was sleek. But the face that greeted us was bright red, with a big brown smear across her nose, and wisps of hair were sticking to her cheeks. "Isn't this supposed to be fall?" she demanded. "How come it's November and it's still so hot? Nobody thought to bring a water bottle. We could die of dehydration."

"Justine, we're only a few yards away from my house," I said.

"A few yards? Is that what you call this climb?" she gasped. "If you'd told me we were hiking up Mount Everest, I'd have popped into Eddie Bauer for some mountaineering boots. These are aerobic shoes, you know. They're designed for smooth surfaces, not the surface of the moon."

I exchanged another grin with Roni. "Obviously you're not the outdoor type, Justine," I said.

She tossed back her hair with a hurt look. "I'd like you to know that I've been to the top of Jungfrau Mountain in Switzerland, which is way higher than this little bump. *And* I've been to the bottom of the Grand Canyon and back."

"But you were wearing mountain boots at the time," Roni said. "And you had a Sherpa guide with you."

Justine grinned. "Actually I went to the top of the Jungfrau on a mountain railway, and I did the Grand Canyon on a mule," she confessed.

Justine was getting a lot better about being teased these days. When we'd first met her, on our first day at Alta Mesa High School in Phoenix, we'd thought she was the world's biggest pain. She was absolutely the last person we'd ever want as a friend. Everything she said was either a boast or a put-down. But she'd just kept tagging along. Being the super-nice people that we are, Roni and I hadn't been able to tell her to get lost. Now we'd gotten used to her superior talk.

After all, she couldn't help being rich and spoiled—she'd been brainwashed by the snobs at Sagebrush Academy before she came to Alta Mesa.

Roni and I, on the other hand, had come to Alta Mesa from a tiny elementary school in Oak Creek—which, let me tell you, is definitely out in the boonies. Like Justine, we knew nobody in our huge new freshman class. That's probably why we hadn't told her to get lost right away. It was better to have a snob to talk to than nobody. Then we'd met Karen, and we were happy to know her. She was another outsider, having come from a Catholic girls' school where they wore terrible plaid uniforms. She was kind of shy at first, but we could tell that she was sweet and fun to be with.

So now we were a foursome. We'd taken turns sleeping over at one another's house every Saturday night. We'd even formed a club to help each other get boyfriends. And it had worked, too: we had all met cute, adorable guys, thanks to the Boyfriend Club. Well, to be honest, the Boyfriend Club hadn't actually gotten any of us together, but it had helped in its own weird way! Now Justine had Danny, Karen had James, and Roni had managed to snag Drew Howard, the most popular sophomore in school. I, of course, had Ben.

Not that I'd needed a boyfriend club to get me together with Ben. We'd known each other all our lives. He'd been my brother Todd's best friend since kindergarten, so I hadn't exactly needed a way to meet him. But it had taken the Boyfriend Club to make me see that all these years I'd been secretly in love with him. Now things were great! Or fairly great, anyway. At least, I hoped they were still great.

We'd gone to the Homecoming Dance together a week ago, and that had been truly wonderful, the most memorable night of my life. I smiled just thinking about it—Ben looking handsome in a dark sports coat and tie, me in a new, grown-up, green off-the-shoulder dress. It was the first time I'd ever been to a dance with a date, and it was super! I knew I wouldn't be bothered by creepy guys. Even better, I knew I wouldn't end up standing in a corner by myself all night.

The dance had been extra special because all my friends were there with their dates. Roni had looked absolutely sensational with Drew, and they won the couples limbo contest. Karen had looked sweet, holding James's hand and dancing with her head on his shoulder. But the biggest surprise had been Justine, who'd gone to the dance with Danny, the funny freshman guy she swore she would never look at twice. They had a great time, too. She was finally learning to act like a normal person!

After that perfect evening I think I floated home, convinced that I'd live happily ever after for the rest of my life. I never dreamed that only a few days later I'd hear something that made me wonder if Ben was getting tired of me after all. . . .

"Are we there yet?" Justine's voice cut through my reverie.

"Almost," I told her.

Panting and gasping, we clambered up the last few feet and stood at the top of Spirit Rock. Below us was the sprawling city of Phoenix, merging with Tempe, Scottsdale, and Mesa in one direction and Glendale and Sun City in the other. Immediately below us, at the foot of the rock, were the fields and ranches that still made up Oak Creek. There were new subdivisions amid the fields now, looking as bright and garish as amusement parks on the green-and-brown landscape. I could see my house clearly, just across a field from the rocky desert area that marked the beginning of Spirit Rock Nature Preserve. Farther away, millions of little toy cars streamed down Interstate 10, but up here we couldn't hear them. The only sounds were the sigh of the wind among the tumbled rocks and the occasional cry of a bird of prey. And, although I wasn't alone this time, I felt what I always felt when I climbed Spirit Rock—that I had somehow managed to pass into another world.

"Look, guys," I said, pointing toward the distant western hills, where the sun now hung like a fat red ball. The sky looked as if it had been streaked with a giant paintbrush—deep red against light blue. As we watched, the sun sank behind the jagged silhouette of the hills and left the world in glowing pink twilight. Although I had seen this a million times before, I sighed with satisfaction. "Okay, so was it worth it?" I asked.

"It sure was," Roni said.

"I guess so," Justine admitted grudgingly.

"It really was," Karen said, her face no longer tired but glowing like the sky. "It's like in a movie—an old Western movie. I keep expecting to see Indians on the horizon."

"You feel the same way I do," I said. "I always feel like I've stepped into another time when I'm up here. Those cars on the freeway don't even matter anymore. You know, Indians really did use Spirit Rock once. I used to collect arrowheads up here—I'll show you when we get home. I was really into Native American culture when I was nine or ten. In fact, I used to come up here and pretend I was an Indian princess."

"You, an Indian princess?" Justine crowed. She had recovered enough to stop panting and was back to her usual tactless self. "You're not the type I'd expect to be a princess, Ginger! Now if you'd said you pretended to be an Indian warrior . . ."

"Okay," I interrupted. "I know I used to be a tomboy. But my princess wasn't at all wimpy. She used to vault onto horses and come galloping down Spirit Rock to lead her people into battle."

"That sounds more like you," Roni said, giving me a knowing smile. "You were always ready to fight for a cause. Remember how you beat up Eddie Pena when he kept trying to take the bow out of my hair?"

Roni looked at the others. "She packed a mean punch in elementary school. That's the only reason I became her friend—I figured it would be better to have someone like that as a friend than an enemy."

"Roni! You make me sound like a female wrestler or something. I was really quiet in elementary school. Nobody knew I existed—"

"Unless something made you mad enough to spring into action," Roni finished. "But I never knew you pretended to be a warrior princess. And I never knew you came up here a lot."

"I never told anybody," I said, "but I always came up here when I was upset, or when I just wanted to be alone. You know what it's like in my house. It was worse when my older brother Steve was still home. He and my brother Todd were always teasing me and there was nobody I could talk to. So I came up here."

"I can see why," Karen said. "I wish I'd had a Spirit Rock near my house. I'd have climbed it every day—if my parents hadn't freaked out about it, of course. You know what they're like. I have to file a flight plan every time I leave the house. But it's like a total escape up here. All the problems of the real world seem far away."

"Exactly," I said. "I know it's silly, but the air seems clearer up here. It's easier to breathe."

"Maybe for you," Justine said. "I'm still getting my breath back from that climb. I didn't realize how out of shape I was. I guess that's the result of no real workouts since I left Sagebrush. PE at Alta Mesa is a joke. At Sagebrush I had fencing, and ballet, and aerobics, and tennis, and skiing in the winter. I was in superb shape—toned, muscled . . . a human goddess."

She frowned as the rest of us started giggling.

"Justine, the human goddess! I love it," Roni said.

"Well, I'm sure Danny thinks she's a goddess," Karen said kindly. She's about the nicest person I've ever met. She doesn't like it when we tease Justine. Usually I don't like teasing people either—after all, I had enough of it from my brothers to know it doesn't feel good—but Justine certainly asks for it sometimes. When she gets into her bragging mode, we have to stop her somehow.

"I'll have to get in shape before ski season," Justine said. "Danny and I have already planned to go skiing together. He's such a terrific athlete. Did I tell you he scored four goals in the last soccer game?"

"Justine, we were there, remember?" I said. "You dragged us along to watch Danny being brilliant on the soccer field before we went to watch Drew being brilliant on the football field—"

"—and then Ben and Todd sitting brilliantly on the bench for their game," Roni finished for me.

I frowned at her. I could say mean things about my brother, but nobody else was allowed to. And nobody in the universe was allowed to say mean things about Ben!

"That's not fair," I snapped. "The coach isn't giving them a chance. Just because they transferred in as juniors and he didn't watch them play last year, he thinks they can't do anything. The one time he tried Ben at wide receiver Ben made a brilliant catch, but the coach took him out on the very next play."

"Okay, Ginger, keep your cool," Roni said, putting a hand on my shoulder. "We all know that Ben is really the world's best football player, as well as being sweet, sensitive, smart, and having the cutest eyelashes of any guy alive."

"Not to mention perfect in every other way not mentioned above," Justine added.

"And Ginger's adoring slave," Karen finished.

They were all grinning at me, so I forced myself to smile back. They really believed that Ben and I were made for each other, that it was love with a capital *L*. Until a couple of days ago, I had thought so, too. Now I wasn't so sure. But I couldn't make myself open my mouth to tell them my fears. The old Ginger, the one who had climbed Spirit Rock to get away from hurts and worries, still hadn't learned to open up completely to her friends. How could I tell them doubts and fears that I didn't even want to admit to myself?

Below us, the lights had come on in the city, and it twinkled like a second sky. "We should go down before it gets dark," I said. "It gets kind of hard to see the path."

"Yeah, and I don't want to fall over a precipice, or get lost in the wilderness," Justine added quickly.

I grinned. "Only Justine could take a little hill with a few rocks on top and turn it into the Alps," I said. "You have a very creative brain, Justine."

"There were precipices on the way up here. I saw them," Justine insisted.

"Any glaciers?" Roni teased.

"Very funny!"

"Wait," Karen said in a low voice, touching my arm gently. "Somebody's down there."

"Two men," Justine agreed. "They're standing on the path."

"It's okay," I said, trying to sound more confident than I felt. "Lots of people come out here to go hiking or walk their dogs."

"I don't see any dog and they're not hiking," Roni whispered. "It looks like they're just standing by the path, waiting."

I swallowed hard. Spirit Rock had seemed only a few yards from my house and civilization before. Now the lights of my street were hopelessly far away and it was getting darker by the minute. In all the times I had come up here alone, I'd never felt scared, but now my friends' fear was rubbing off on me.

"Don't worry. There are four of us," I said. "And we're not exactly wimps. Just ask Eddie Pena."

"I wish those men weren't just standing there," Karen said.

"Now one of them's crouching down behind a bush," Justine whispered. "Is there another way we could go back?"

"This is the only real path," I said. "In the daylight it's easy enough to cut straight down through the rocks, but it's getting kind of dark now."

"Get in pairs and we'll march down past them," Roni said. "Maybe they'll think we're *all* female wrestlers."

We giggled nervously. Then we set out down the

path, walking briskly and swinging our arms. As we got close to the men, we heard one of them speak.

"We'd better call it quits, Harry. I can't see a thing anymore. Let's leave it."

Suddenly the big shape of the second man rose up right beside us, making Justine scream and grab me so hard that I almost lost my balance.

"Go on, tell them we're armed and dangerous," she hissed in my ear.

The second man stepped out onto the path. "I'm sorry, did I scare you?" he said. Up close, he looked like a normal father type, dressed in a shirt and tie. "You probably didn't see me because I was bending down, looking through the surveying instrument."

"You're making a survey of this area?" Roni asked. "They're not planning to put a new freeway through or something, are they?"

Both men laughed. "Nothing like that," the first man said. "It's going to be part of a new resort called Mountain Shadows—very upscale, we're told! The hotel itself is going to be built just about here, with the view. Then there'll be a golf course and a mall."

I didn't think I was hearing right. "Wait a minute," I said. "You can't build a resort here. This is a nature preserve."

"Not anymore, I guess," the first man said. "I don't know much about it, but the plans are all in place to go ahead with the resort. We're putting in the stakes for the site of the hotel now."

"But you can't do that!" I yelled. "Nobody told me about it. Nobody gave me a chance to tell them my opinion."

The men looked more amused than embarrassed. "Sorry, honey, but it's nothing to do with me," one of them said. "We're just hired by the developers."

"But this is public land. It belongs to people like me. Where are we supposed to go if this is a golf course? Aren't there enough golf courses in Scottsdale? There has to be some mistake." I could hear myself yelling now.

"Hey, keep your hair on, little lady," the second man said. "We're just the surveyors."

"Then you can stop surveying," I snapped, "because there isn't going to be any golf course or resort or mall. I'm going home to stop it right now!"

The second man laughed. Roni sensed I was about to lose it completely and took a firm hold of my arm. "Come on, Ginger, let's go home," she said calmly. "If it's going to be a resort, there's nothing we can do."

"Oh yeah?" I demanded. "Well, you just watch me. Because this is *my* Spirit Rock and I'm not going to let them put in some dumb resort. I'm going to stop them if it's the last thing I do!"

2

My friends practically had to drag me home. I think they were afraid I was going to run around Spirit Rock pulling up all the little stakes the men had put in. The way I was feeling, I might have done it, too! I was so angry that I was like a volcano about to blow its top. As we walked across the fields, I tried to see if my dad's truck was outside our house. I needed him to be home right now. He'd know about things like property developers. He'd know if they were allowed just to walk onto a public mountain and start putting a stupid golf course there!

As we got closer to the house I saw that not just one, but two trucks were in the driveway. The new black shiny one was my dad's. The beat-up old red one was Ben's.

"Todd and Ben are back from football practice," I said, breaking into a run.

"Oh, everything's okay, then," I heard Justine comment behind me. "Ben will go up the mountain and single-handedly defeat the evil developers for the love of Ginger."

I didn't have the energy to think of a good put-down. In fact, I was secretly hoping Ben *would* come up with a way to stop the developers. And if Ben couldn't, then I hoped my dad would. I spent most of my life battling the old-fashioned men around me and letting them know that I was as good as they were in every way. But right now, I wanted my dad and my brother and Ben to take over for me. I wanted them to say, "Don't worry, we'll handle this. We'll stop those guys from putting in a resort."

As I rushed through the front door, three startled faces looked up from the TV set.

"You've got to do something right now!" I burst out. "Stop them!"

My father and Ben jumped to their feet.

"What is it, honey?" Dad asked.

"Are you okay?" Ben was at my side.

"Maybe some Martians want to take her away in

their spaceship," Todd quipped. "Nah—they have better taste in women on Mars."

"Shut up," I snapped. It was incredible how my brother always had to start in with his stupid teasing, especially when Ben was around.

My friends trooped into the room behind me.

"Ginger's really upset," Roni said, putting her arm around my shoulders.

I had recovered enough to talk by now. "We were up on Spirit Rock," I explained to my father, "and we saw some men up there . . ."

"Did they bother you?" Ben demanded.

"No," I said, "it wasn't like that." I was close to tears, but I managed to steady my voice. "They're going to build a resort there, with a golf course."

All three males in the room burst out laughing.

"That's the big drama?" Todd said, giving my dad one of his "Ginger-is-a-lunatic" looks.

"It's not funny!" I yelled. I glared at Ben, who managed to stop laughing.

"We thought you were in some kind of trouble," he explained.

"We're all in trouble," I said. "Don't you realize what I'm saying? They're putting in a golf course and a big hotel and a mall up on Spirit Rock."

"All right!" Todd said. "You know what that means, don't you? We get to caddy at a golf course right near home—no more trekking out to Scottsdale. Think of all those twenty-buck tips!" He turned and gave Ben a high five.

I was getting angrier by the minute. Now my own family was turning traitor on me! "Wait a minute!" I shouted. "Is that all you can think about? You're willing to trade the beauty of Spirit Rock for lousy twenty-buck tips?"

Todd and Ben looked at each other. "Yep," they both agreed.

"After all," Ben said, "it's not that beautiful. I mean, it has a nice view, but it's just scrub at the bottom. And it's not as if many people go there. There are other county parks with better cactus displays. Spirit Rock doesn't have picnic grounds or anything. I think a golf course will be an improvement."

"He's right, honey," my father said. "It will be kind of nice to look out the windows and see green all year round, instead of that dirty, rocky landscape. And it could be worse. They could have put condos all over it."

"It will upgrade the whole community," Todd said. "Use your head for once, Ginger. The kind of people who use a golf resort will bring in a lot of money. Besides, you should be happy to have a mall out here. You're the one who's always complaining you have to go all the way into Scottsdale to find real stores."

"I'd give up every store in the world if I could keep Spirit Rock," I said. "How can they have done this without telling anybody, Dad?"

My father shrugged. "I guess they must have applied for all the necessary permits."

"But don't they have to ask our opinion first?" I demanded.

"I suppose they had to have a public hearing at some stage, but they could have slipped it into the middle of any council meeting," my father said. "These big developers are pretty slick operators. They usually get what they want."

"Not this time," I said. "Dad, I want you to find out how we can stop this."

My father smiled helplessly at my friends, hoping, I think, that they'd all agree I had flipped out.

"My dad works in the county planning department," Roni said. "He could find out what to do . . . and he'd know whether the developer got all the right permits."

"Do you think he'd do that for us?" I asked, looking hopefully at Roni.

"Sure," she said. "I mean, if my best friend can't watch the sunset anymore—"

"Or pretend she's an Indian princess," Justine added.

Trust Justine. She never knows when to keep her

mouth shut. Todd picked up on it instantly. "An Indian princess? See, Ben, I told you my sister was screwy!"

"That was way back when I was a little kid," I said, flushing pink as I felt Ben's eyes on me. I waited for him to say something nice, like he'd always thought I was natural and untamed like an Indian princess, but he didn't.

"So Roni, can your dad look into it when he goes to work tomorrow?" I went on, trying to pretend that none of the males in the room existed. "We could call him from the pay phone at lunchtime."

"Ginger, give it a break," Todd drawled from the chair where he was sprawled. "If they're building this golf course, there's nothing you can do. Obviously they got permission first. You don't start building a resort and hope nobody will notice."

"Maybe that's just what they thought," I said. "And maybe nobody *would* have noticed except me. But those developers are going to be in for a big surprise! Now they've got Ginger Hartman to deal with."

This made Todd burst out laughing again. Even my dad grinned.

My cheeks were so hot that you could toast marshmallows on them. "Fine," I said. "It doesn't matter if nobody else cares about this. I care and I'm going to do something. You just wait until you find parking meters outside the house. You wait until they dig up your baseball diamond because they want to put in a putting green. Then you'll wish you'd listened to me."

My friends were looking at one another uneasily. "Um, I guess we should be getting home, Ginger," Karen said. "I still have math homework to do."

"And I need to give my nails a hot wax treatment after getting all that dust on them," Justine agreed.

They headed for the door. I followed them out. Roni touched my arm. "Don't worry too much. I'll talk to my dad about it," she said.

"I'm sorry you're so upset," Karen added.

"Thanks." I managed a smile.

"It might all turn out for the best," Justine said. "Maybe they'll put in a tramway to the top of Spirit Rock, so you won't have to climb up that crazy path anymore."

I knew she was trying to be helpful, and I had to laugh. "Justine, you don't get it, do you? I don't think anybody gets it except me. I like Spirit Rock because it's the way it is: nobody goes there and it's wild and it's a hard climb up to the top. If they put in a tramway, they'd probably put in a restaurant at the top and telescopes all around and it would become a tourist attraction!"

"But that would be great, wouldn't it?" Justine said.

"Justine, it's time we went home." Karen took her

arm. "See you in the morning, Ginger. Thanks for letting us study at your house."

"See ya," I said, waving as they set off down the street. It was almost dark, and Spirit Rock loomed behind my house like a sleeping dinosaur. I imagined it glowing with floodlights and echoing with music, and I shuddered.

"What are you doing all alone out in the dark?" Ben's deep voice came from behind me. He put a hand on my shoulder. "I'm sorry," he said softly. "I guess I helped upset you in there."

"It's just that nobody seemed to understand why I was upset," I said. "*You* even laughed."

"I know. I'm sorry," he said again. "I guess Spirit Rock isn't special to me the way it is to you. If you want to know the truth, I don't even like the place."

"Why not?"

"I have bad memories. When I was little, right after I joined the Cub Scouts, we went on a hike up Spirit Rock. I fell down and skinned my knee." He frowned at the memory. "That wasn't the worst part! My backpack had all my food in it, plus my jacket—it was so heavy that I couldn't get up again. I called, but nobody heard me."

I started to giggle at the image of Ben trapped on the ground in his Cub Scout uniform.

"To top it all off," he continued, "I was sitting on

an ants' nest. There were all these ants crawling on me, and my knee was bleeding, and I thought everyone else had gone and left me. And I'd just read a book about soldier ants that can eat big animals down to skeletons in minutes. I was totally freaked out by the time they found me . . . Hey," he added. "What's so funny? That's not fair. You got mad when I laughed at you."

"Your story is funny," I said. "You have to admit it's funnier than mine."

"I guess you're right," he said, caressing my neck with his hand. He was smiling down at me with those warm, gentle eyes I like so much. I started to melt the way I always did when he looked at me, until suddenly I remembered that I was mad at him.

"So," I said, trying to sound breezy, "how was the party last night?"

The smile froze on his face. "How did you know about the party?"

"Hey, I'm not entirely stupid," I said. "You told me it was a football get-together to watch game films. Todd didn't get back until after midnight. I don't think Coach's pep talks go on that late."

"It was pretty boring, actually," he said. "I thought of asking you, but I didn't think it was your kind of thing."

"Sure," I said. It wasn't what I wanted to say at all.

I wanted to say, "I heard you in the locker room on Friday night. The window was open and you didn't know I was waiting outside. I heard your football buddies tell you about the party and how wild it was going to be."

"Coral Hotchkiss is going to be there, and those friends of hers from Tempe," the voice from the locker room had said. Then there were wolf whistles and the sort of dumb comments guys make when they think they're being macho studs. Then Todd laughed and said, "Too bad, Ben, my kid sister probably won't let you go. . . . You guys know Ben's dating my little sister, right?" More laughter and then Ben's voice. "Give me a break, guys. We're just . . . like . . . friends. It's not like she's my girlfriend or anything. She's a nice kid, but I don't have to ask her permission."

Later that evening Ben had told me that the coach wanted the team to get together on Saturday night to watch game films. He actually lied to me! I wanted to ask, "Don't you love me anymore? How can you want to go to a party with a bunch of Tempe cheerleaders if you really care about me?"

I still wanted to ask it, but I couldn't. I was too scared that he would give me the wrong answer. So I said in my carefree voice, "Too bad the party was boring. I guess I better go in and help with dinner."

"Yeah, I'm on my way home, too," he said. "I've

got a ton of homework to do. See you tomorrow."

"Okay," I said.

He brought my face toward his and touched my forehead gently with his lips. I wondered if that was his way of saying it was over between us.

As I watched him climb into his truck, I found myself wondering *what,* exactly, was over. It had always worried me that I didn't really know how Ben felt about me. I mean, after we decided we liked each other, we hadn't decided anything else. At least, we never got to the stage I'd always dreamed of.

We'd gone to movies together. He held my hand at school sometimes. I sat behind the players' bench and cheered him at football games. He kissed me good night when he brought me home. And all this was great. But he had never come out and asked me to be his special girl. He had never announced to the world that he and I were a couple. In fact, judging by that conversation in the locker room, he went to a lot of trouble to make it sound like we *weren't* a couple.

I closed my eyes, as if it was too painful to watch the taillights of his truck fading away down the road. It was almost a physical ache in my heart to realize that I might have lost him.

I should have known it was too good to last, I thought. Maybe he'd only been interested in me because he was new at a big school and he hadn't known any girls yet. I couldn't expect a junior, especially a junior on the football team, to keep on dating a freshman nobody, could I? It just wasn't realistic. Except that this was Ben. And I knew now that I'd loved him since I was five years old.

3

Monday did not start well. The English test we'd spent all Sunday studying for turned out to be super hard. There was only one tiny section on *Tom Sawyer*, which was the book we had been reading for the past month, and a whole big section on vocabulary, which took me by surprise. There was a ton of long words, and we had to put them all into sentences. I spent a scary half hour trying to decide if it was "commiserate for" or "commiserate with." By the time I handed my paper in, I was sure I'd bombed. But judging by the faces around me as we left the classroom, most of the other students felt the same.

"Was that unfair or what?" Roni demanded loudly the moment we were through the classroom door.

"Didn't she tell us that the test would be on *Tom Sawyer*?" She glanced back at Mrs. Lopez's desk, hoping she'd heard.

"She sort of hinted it," Karen agreed.

"I'd never even heard half of those vocabulary words," Roni moaned. "I mean, if she was going to give us a vocabulary test, why didn't she give us a list to study?"

"Apparently all those words were in the books we've read this year," Karen explained.

"But that would mean we'd actually have to have read the books!" Justine looked horrified. "Doesn't the woman know about Cliff Notes?"

"Justine!" Karen said, laughing. "We *are* supposed to have read the books. That's what English class is all about."

Justine tossed back her hair. "It might be okay for you brainy people who like to read," she said. "But it would take me all night to read the chapters she assigned every day. I'm sorry, but I am not giving up watching '90210' to struggle through *Tom Sawyer* when I can read the Cliff Notes in five minutes."

"I read the books," I said, "but I didn't have a clue about half those words. I hope I don't get an *F*. My dad would throw a fit if he thought I was failing a class."

"Mine too," Justine said. "He'd probably hire me a

tutor, and that's the last thing in the world I want. Although, of course, it could be a cute tutor, one who would recognize my obvious intelligence . . ."

"Justine, shut up," I snapped.

"I'm depressed," Roni said. "I say we all go to the cafeteria and get ourselves chocolate shakes."

"Good idea," Justine said. "Christine, my stepmother, is on this real health food kick now that she's pregnant. Nothing with additives. Only organically grown veggies. I think I have a multigrain bun with alfalfa sprouts in my lunch bag." She made a gagging face.

"You could make your own lunch, Justine," I said.

Justine looked surprised. "Then I'd have to get up fifteen minutes earlier," she said. "I already have to get up at seven to have enough time to wash my hair and choose my outfit and put on my makeup."

I looked at Roni and grinned. How very different other people's lives were, I decided. My morning routine took about fifteen minutes, max. Just enough time to run through the shower, comb my hair, grab the nearest pair of jeans and a T-shirt, throw a bagel and an apple into a bag, and run out the door. I'd never worn makeup to school, or taken the time to style my hair, or even given much thought to my clothes.

Suddenly I thought of something horrible. Was

that why Ben was getting tired of me? Maybe I didn't look good enough. Maybe I didn't look sexy enough. But makeup and frilly clothes just weren't me. And Ben wouldn't want me to be someone I wasn't . . . would he?

The subject was too painful to think about. I dragged my mind away from Ben and remembered my other big worry. "Roni, we were going to call your dad at lunch, weren't we?"

"Oh, yeah," she said. "Okay, let's do it. We'll meet you guys in the cafeteria, since it's raining out. Save us a seat."

"Fat chance of that," Karen said. "You know what it's like trying to find a seat in the cafeteria, but we'll do our best. I'll get Justine to lie down on a bench."

"Me? Lie down?" Justine demanded as we walked away. "Do you know what sort of gunk gets spilled on those benches? You want me to put my head on someone's dried chili?"

The call to Roni's dad at his office didn't take long. He told us that Spirit Rock was now part of the land that had been annexed to the city last summer. That meant city hall would have granted the permits.

I glared at Roni as she told me this. "I bet that was the whole reason behind the city annexing our part of Oak Creek," I said. "The developers wanted to build this resort and they knew that the county wouldn't let them, but the city wouldn't care. I'm going over to city hall right after school today."

Roni looked sympathetic, but she shook her head. "Why don't you give up on this, Ginger? It's crazy. You're a kid. You can't stop some big development company from putting in a resort."

"I don't care," I said. "For the first time in my life I've found something that really matters to me, and I'm not prepared to give up without a fight. After all, that's what democracy is all about, isn't it?"

"In theory," Roni said. "But I kind of get the feeling that when you've got the money and you know the right people, you get what you want."

"But that's wrong!" I yelled, loudly enough for a group of upperclassmen to turn around and stare at us. "That has to be changed."

"Ginger, the Caped Crusader." Roni giggled. "I really admire the way you're going at this, but I don't see what you can do."

"I don't know either," I said, "but there must be something. Maybe I'll discover something at city hall that the developers are doing wrong . . . putting in an illegal sewer line or using too much water. There must be something. . . ." My voice trailed off. I had no idea what that "something" could be. Right now my only idea for stopping the developers was to lie down in front of the first bulldozer. And I had a weird feeling that it might just run over me!

After school I caught the bus to the Phoenix city hall. I was pretty scared about going alone, because city hall was huge and I wasn't even that comfortable wandering around the city by myself. But Roni had made it clear that she thought going to city hall was stupid and useless. So I didn't have much choice. Maybe Karen or Justine would have come with me, if I'd begged them, but I wasn't the sort of person who begged. I'd always liked to be independent. I guess growing up with no mother and two older brothers had made me expect to do things for myself. My mother died when I was three—too young to remember anything more than a couple of songs she sang to me. Since then I've gotten used to being alone.

But as I left the bus and stood in front of the big, imposing building, I really wished I hadn't been so independent. I had to force myself to go up the steps and in through the big, revolving door. The porter at the information desk was very nice, and I soon found myself in the planning department. The woman there looked like the librarian at my school. She always made you feel that libraries would run more smoothly if they didn't let students touch the books. This woman gave me the same feeling—that city hall would work much better if they kept the public out of it. A sign on her desk said MS. H. BRAITHWAITE.

"What is it, honey?" she asked in a phony-sweet voice. "If this is some kind of school project, we're real busy in here right now."

"It isn't a school project," I said. "I need information on the new golf resort that's being built on Spirit Rock. I think it's going to be called Mountain Shadows."

"Oh, yes, the Mountain Shadows project," she said, smiling. "That's a very big one—golf course, mall, everything you could want. What did you need to know about it?"

"How they got permission to build on a public nature preserve without telling anyone," I said, my voice rising.

The phony smile disappeared from her face. "There was no need for public hearings in this case," she said. "The area was never officially designated either a county park or a public nature preserve. It was merely county open space land, which then became city open space land. And now it's up to the city to do what they like with it." Her eyes met mine and they were ice cold. I returned her stare. She wasn't going to scare me.

"So who decided to sell the land without telling anyone?" I demanded. "Aren't taxpayers supposed to know what's being done in their city? Shouldn't they be able to express their opinions?"

"Shouldn't you leave a matter like this to your parents?" Ms. H. Braithwaite said, attempting another smile that didn't reach her eyes. "After all, you're not a taxpayer yet, are you? So it's really none of your concern."

"For all you know, my father might be a very important taxpayer," I said. "He might have all kinds of important friends, too."

She blinked at this, as if she realized it might be true. I wondered what she'd say if she found out my father serviced farm equipment.

"The transaction would have been discussed at a regular city council meeting, I'm sure," she said. "Those meetings are all open to the public, and the minutes are available for your inspection at the city clerk's office. Now, if you'll excuse me, I have a lot of work to get finished tonight."

She looked back down at her desk.

"And if I wanted to protest this resort, who would I go to?"

"I'm afraid it's a little late for that," she said. "You should have been present at the meeting when it was discussed. Now that the council has voted on it, all the necessary permits have been granted. Thank you so much for stopping by, honey." She got up and went into a back office, closing the door behind her. There was nothing I could do, apart from tearing her filing cabinets to pieces, but go back downstairs and head for home.

When I got off the bus at my street, I looked up at the horizon. There it was, silhouetted against the clear, evening skyline . . . Spirit Rock, looking more beautiful and mysterious than ever. I felt as if I could hear it calling me, as if it had a life of its own. "I'm counting on you, Ginger," it seemed to be saying. "You're the only one who can help me now."

"But I can't do anything," I blurted out loud. "I don't know what to do. I've never had to do anything like this before. I don't know where to start!"

I threw my book bag into the carport and headed out across the field. I had to climb Spirit Rock now. Maybe if I stood on the summit and felt the magic flowing into me one more time, I'd get an inspiration on what to do next.

There were no surveyors at the base of the hill, but their little stakes and flags fluttered on both sides of the path. I imagined a big glass-and-concrete building rearing up in front of me, and I shuddered. I thought I felt the hill shudder with me. I ran through the forest of stakes and flags until the red rocks of the summit began and the path became too steep and rocky to go fast.

As I climbed, the breeze met me, smelling fresh and herb scented—not at all like the car exhaust smells that were always in the city air below. All sounds melted away except the wind sighing through the rocks. I came out onto a little platform and stood still, letting the rock work its magic. I closed my eyes and felt the tension drain away, just like it always did up here. I was free, floating with the breeze, part of the world of nature, where offices and council meetings and permits didn't matter at all. Spirit Rock dreamed on, seemingly unworried about what was going to happen to it.

I remembered how I had stood here as a little kid, pretending I was Eagle Feather, princess and ruler of the tribe, watching over my people. I would jump on my snow-white pony and gallop down the rock to defend them against all enemies. I tried to picture it again now—the valley full of campfires, the braves ready to ride to war, but it was no use. I couldn't make the city disappear.

How simple everything had seemed then. I bet Princess Eagle Feather wouldn't have found it easy if she'd had to fight Ms. H. Braithwaite. It was no use. That world of make-believe was gone forever. Maybe Spirit Rock wasn't a magic place after all.

As I turned to head back down the path I got the feeling that someone was watching me. I looked up into the rocks and almost lost my footing, I was so scared. A young brave was sitting there, up among the rocks. His handsome profile glowed bronze in the rays of the setting sun. His black hair shone, almost dark blue like a bird's feathers. He was wearing a fringed buckskin jacket and he was staring at me, unblinking. There was something familiar about him.

Okay, I thought, *I've finally flipped out. I've had too much stress and now I'm hallucinating.*

"Hi," I said, my voice a nervous squeak.

"Hi," he said. "I know you, don't I?"

This is it, my brain was saying. *I've entered the twilight zone. He's one of those spirit messengers, sent to take me back into the past.*

"You do?" My voice was still a squeak.

"Yeah," he said. "We pass each other in the hall sometimes."

In what hall? The hallways of the twilight zone? I must still have been staring at him with a dumb expression on my face, because he went on, "Don't you go to Alta Mesa? You have health ed in room 105, right? I see you coming out when I'm waiting for world history."

My school? He went to my school! That's why I recognized him. It was just that I'd never thought of his being a Native American before.

The boy stood up from the rock he was sitting on and jumped down beside me. I could see now that under the buckskin jacket he was wearing a

Suns T-shirt and jeans. "I'm Johnny Edwards," he said.

"Hi, Ginger Hartman," I answered, smiling weakly. "You gave me a shock sitting up there in the rocks. I thought I was seeing a ghost."

"Sorry," he said. "You gave me a shock, too. I didn't think anybody else came up here."

"I used to, all the time," I said. "My house is down there at the end of the street. I used to come up here to think."

"Me too," he said. "I like this place. I really feel I can get away from all the pressure up here. It's so quiet and peaceful."

"Not for much longer," I said. "You've heard what they're planning to do, haven't you?"

"No, what?"

"You didn't see the little stakes at the bottom of the hill?"

"I thought they were some sort of Boy Scout obstacle course."

"They're to mark out a big luxury golf resort and hotel."

"You're kidding!"

"No, I'm not."

"They can't do that."

"That's what I said, but it seems they can. I went to city hall today. The woman there more or less told me to get lost."

"But there was nothing about it in the papers," he

said, glaring at me angrily. "Don't they have to get permits and things? They can't just take away open space."

"They've got all the permits they need. The city council voted on them," I said.

He sighed. "Just another example of the native peoples being cheated out of their ancestral lands," he said.

"This really was an ancient Indian site?" I asked excitedly.

"Native American," he corrected me. "Indians live in India."

"Sorry," I said. "I never seem to get that right."

"It's okay. Most people don't. And yes, it's definitely a site that figures in my tribe's history."

"I knew it. When I was a little kid, I found things I was sure were arrowheads."

"Projectile points," he corrected. "Real arrowheads were very small. Most of the things they call arrowheads are really projectile points."

"Projectile points, then," I said. "But you really think that ancient tribes used to come here?"

"Why do you think it's called Spirit Rock?" he asked. "I'm from the Pima tribe. The medicine man used to come up here to speak with the spirits."

"That's the answer!" I said excitedly. "They can't build on an old holy site, can they?"

Johnny smiled. "Unfortunately, most of the hills around here were holy sites of one kind or another. It's really hard to prove—city councils don't go for tribal legends. And most of the time the native peoples didn't disturb the rock in any way, so there's no evidence."

"So you don't think we could prove Spirit Rock was holy?"

"I doubt it," he said. "And most of the modern Pima would rather have a golf course."

I looked out over the stream of rush-hour traffic stopped on Interstate 10. "So it's hopeless, then."

"You really care about this, don't you?" Johnny asked softly.

I nodded. "This place is special to me. I didn't realize how special until I saw them putting in those stakes for the resort."

"We could try to do something," he said. "There's an ecology club at school. They're very active in saving the desert tortoise from off-road vehicles and all that sort of stuff. Maybe they'd know how to stop the golf course."

A thin ray of hope shone through my gloom. "You really think so?"

He gave me an encouraging smile. "It's worth a try," he said. "Come on, it will be dark soon. I have to get home by sunset."

"You have ceremonies then?" I asked reverently.

He grinned. "No. Reruns of '*Star Trek: The Next Generation*,'" he said, and loped ahead of me down the steep path.

4

"Any luck at city hall?" Roni asked me on the bus to school the next morning. I shook my head. "I didn't think so," she said. "My dad said he's dealt with Cromer and Ferndale, the developers, before. He says they're mega-big and they know how to pull all the right strings."

"Yeah, well, they never came up against Ginger the Caped Crusader before," I said, flexing my biceps.

Roni laughed. "You're not going to drop this, are you?"

"No way. And now I've found someone to help me fight city hall."

"Who?"

"The ideal person—an Indian brave. Oops! I mean, a Native American."

Roni looked worried. "Ginger, you're not going back into that Indian princess fantasy, are you?"

"No, Roni, I mean it. I went up on Spirit Rock and I met a real Pima Indian up there."

Roni was still smiling. "You're not putting me on, are you?"

"Cross my heart," I said. "His name's Johnny Edwards and he goes to our school. I think he must be a sophomore, because he has world history in the room we have for health ed. Anyway, he's going to take me to the ecology club at school today to get their help."

"What can they do?"

I shrugged. "I don't know. But maybe they'll have some ideas. Johnny says they've been great at getting other projects stopped when they were damaging the environment. Maybe they know how to get the right publicity."

Roni shrugged. "But if the permits have been granted, it doesn't matter what the newspapers say. The city council isn't going to change its mind."

"We'll see," I said. "I have to be hopeful and I have to keep on working at this."

"It's to keep your mind off Ben, isn't it?" Roni asked quietly.

I jumped. "Excuse me?"

"Ben and you—I know," she said.

"You know what?" I demanded.

"That things aren't going too great," she said. She chewed on her lip, a sure sign that she was nervous. "Karen and I have been debating whether to tell you this, but I think maybe you should know. Ben didn't go to a football meeting on Saturday night. He went to a big, wild party. Drew told me."

"I know," I said.

"You know? Weren't you mad?"

"Pretty mad," I said. "Actually more scared than mad."

"How come you didn't say anything to us about it? We're your friends, you know."

"I know," I said. "I didn't want to talk about it to anyone. It was like it wasn't real as long as I didn't say it out loud."

"So you haven't even confronted Ben with it and asked him why he was a crummy, two-timing, lying jerk?"

"I told him I knew," I said.

"And?"

"And he said that the party wasn't my thing. That's why he hadn't mentioned it."

"Creep," Roni said.

"He's not a creep," I said quickly. "At least, I hope he's not a creep. I suppose I should have known . . ."

"Known what?"

"He's a junior, Roni. I should have known he'd get tired of dating a freshman when he got to know more people around school."

She frowned at me. "That's really negative, Ginger. Don't put yourself down. You're cute and fun and nice. Anyway, plenty of upperclassmen date younger people. And you and Ben were so right for each other. *Are* so right for each other."

"I thought so, too," I said. It came out scarcely louder than a whisper. I felt a big lump in my throat, and I swallowed hard. "Oh, Roni, what am I going to do to get him back?" I said. "I don't want to lose him. I thought this was my dream romance, but now I'm not sure anymore. I mean, it never turned into the wonderful relationship I thought it would. Ben never told anyone that we're going together. He doesn't invite me to football parties. That must mean he doesn't care very much, right?"

"I'm sure he cares, Ginger," Roni said. "You only have to see the way he looks at you."

I sighed. "Sometimes I think he's just being nice to me because he feels like my big brother."

"Some big brother," Roni said, grinning. "Those are not brotherly looks he gives you."

"So why would he lie to me about a party? Why would he want to go with all those girls?"

"He's a guy," Roni said simply. "There's something

in every guy's brain that goes gaga over the thought of sexy females. It's just a genetic flaw, I guess."

"I hope that's all it was," I said. "But I get the feeling that the rest of the guys on the team are trying to fix Ben and Todd up with girls who hang out with them. They were teasing him about dating me. He even said that we were just friends—"

"He told you that?"

"No, I overheard them talking in the locker room."

"Maybe he is a creep after all, Ginger," Roni said. "Maybe you're better off without him. My advice is to play it cool for a while—like I did when I wasn't sure of Drew."

"Roni!" I exclaimed, laughing loud enough to make the people sitting in front of us turn around and stare. "When you weren't sure about Drew, you acted like the world had come to an end."

"So do what I say, not what I do," she said. "And I say make him jealous. Show him you don't care if he goes to a stupid party or not."

"I don't know how to make him jealous." I shook my head. "It's not as if I've got guys lined up fighting over me."

"You could have, if you had the right image," Roni said. "You still don't care much about your appearance."

"Thanks a lot."

"No, I meant that in a positive way," she said,

grinning. "What I meant was that you don't get up at six-thirty like Justine to do your nails and your makeup."

"That's true," I admitted. "And I suppose you're right about appearance. I grab the first clothes I find in the morning. I don't even coordinate outfits. But that's just the way I am. I've always been a tomboy. Remember, I never had a mother to dress me in frilly dresses like you did."

"Be thankful for that," Roni said. "I always felt like a total dork. If I could have changed out of those dumb dresses on the way to school, I would have."

"I thought you looked nice," I said. "I always envied you."

"I always envied your shorts and T-shirts."

We looked at each other and laughed.

"I guess nobody is ever happy with the way they look," I said.

"Except Justine. She thinks she looks perfect all the time." Roni giggled.

"So you really think I should make a big effort to look sexy around school and get guys interested in me?"

"Not necessarily sexy," Roni said. "You have to be yourself. But you might try looking like a girl who's cute and bubbly and fun to know—which you are. Plenty of guys will like you then."

"The only guys we know are the nerds," I said,

"and I don't want to appear attractive to them!"

The nerds were a group of weird, computer-loving social outcasts with bad hair who had latched on to us at the beginning of the year. They haunted us around school, always showing up when we didn't want them to. In spite of our constantly telling them to get lost, they still kept hoping that their grotesque charm would make us fall for them. By now we were used to it. We even felt fond of them, the same way you might feel about a pet lizard—repulsive, but endearing! Still, I wasn't prepared to be seen with a nerd just to make Ben jealous.

Roni was shaking with laughter. "If Ben thought you'd been dating a nerd, I don't think he'd want you back," she said. "What about this Johnny Edwards guy? Is he nice?"

"Super nice, but shorter than me," I said. "I don't think I could ever date a guy who was shorter than me."

"I agree," Roni said. "I remember those dances in eighth grade when the boys only came up to our shoulders. Totally embarrassing."

I gazed out of the bus window. "Maybe the ecology club will turn up some new talent," I suggested.

"Nah. Ecology types are too serious. They care more about saving the lesser-spotted banana slug than they do about getting a date. And they dress weird. You'd have to go out and buy yourself boots and hiking shorts."

"You never know," I said. "I'm really hopeful about this club meeting."

"That's what I like—a positive attitude," Roni said. "By the end of the day you'll have stopped the development on Spirit Rock *and* met a new guy."

But I could tell that she didn't really believe it. I didn't believe it either. For one thing, I didn't really want to make Ben jealous. I just wanted Ben, sweet and loving as always, waiting for me after school. Still, as I walked into the ecology club classroom, I found myself scanning the room for possible babes.

Roni was right. There weren't any. She was also right that all the ecology types were very serious. They had a map with pins on it to represent the endangered species that were currently making comebacks. They applauded when they heard that the bald eagle was doing better, and they looked devastated when they heard that the piping plover might now be beyond salvation.

I didn't get off to a good start. I was the only person in the room who didn't know that the piping plover was a bird—and when I saw a picture of it, I commented that it looked like any other small brown bird. Well, it did! Anyway, everyone glared at me as if

I'd just suggested that we have barbecued bald eagle for lunch.

When we'd finished mourning the piping plover, Johnny got up and introduced me. He told the group what was happening out at Spirit Rock. They were instantly interested, and asked a lot of questions. Johnny motioned to me.

"Ginger's the one who's been doing all the research," he said. "She'll tell you what she's found out."

A couple of girls gave me looks that clearly meant, "If she doesn't even know a piping plover when she sees one, can we believe a word she says?" But even they seemed interested when I told them about city hall and the permits being given without any public hearings.

"I think we should wait for Scott," a girl called Elaine said. "He's fought Cromer and Ferndale before. He might know the right way to attack this."

"Yeah, where is Scott?" one of the too-serious boys asked.

"He had a senior class council meeting. He said he'd be here as soon as he could," Elaine replied.

"Lunch hour's half over. Should we wait any longer?" the boy said. "It seems to me that we have to act quickly on this or it will be too late. Once the resort is there, they're not going to take it out again."

"I agree," I said. "They're already putting in stakes and taking measurements."

At that moment the door opened.

"Great, here's Scott now," Elaine said. "Do you know Scott Masters, Ginger? He's the club spokesperson. He's been on TV and everything."

"How's that for an intro? You make me sound like David Letterman," said the new guy.

I turned to look at him, and I think my mouth dropped open. Standing in the doorway was the most gorgeous guy I had ever seen around school. In fact, he was the most gorgeous guy I'd ever seen, period. He was tall—around six two—and rugged looking, with sun-streaked hair and a great tan. And talk about built! Muscles positively rippled under his tank top. What's more, when he looked at me, his bright blue eyes sparkled and his face broke into the most adorable smile. "New member?" he said. "Hi, I'm Scott."

I was glad that Elaine spoke for me. I don't think my tongue would have obeyed me enough to say anything coherent. "This is Ginger," she said. "And you know Johnny, right? They need our help to stop Cromer and Ferndale from putting in a golf resort on Spirit Rock."

Those blue eyes were serious and intense now. "Spirit Rock?" he asked, looking directly at me. "That's out past Oak Creek, right?"

"Right," I managed to say.

"Isn't it a nature preserve?"

I shook my head. "I thought so, but it was never officially registered. It became city land this summer and they sold it to developers. Apparently they didn't need public hearings."

"That's bad," Scott said. "I'm not too familiar with Spirit Rock. Do you know of any rare species growing or living out there?"

He was looking at me intently, and I was thinking about how those blue eyes were fringed with long, dark lashes. Even if the place had been crawling with piping plovers, I wouldn't have been able to think of a single rare species. I desperately wished that I had discovered a little-known plant on Spirit Rock so that I could impress Scott. Too bad I didn't know a dandelion from a mule-ear.

"I haven't done a detailed survey," I heard myself saying. "Maybe the rock has more value as a Pima Indian site. Johnny says it was a holy place."

Scott smiled at me again, almost making me forget that Spirit Rock had ever existed. "Good point," he said. "Maybe Pima archaeological site is the way to go. We'd better take a look. Are you free after school today, Ginger?"

Was I free? Whatever commitment I had, I would have gotten out of it—SATs, detention, shopping spree at the mall, championship volleyball game, date with Ben. . . . I'd have willingly canceled any of them for the chance to be on Spirit Rock with Scott. As it happened, I only had homework and reruns on TV to look forward to anyway.

"I think I can make it," I said, sounding amazingly cool.

"Great," he said. "How about you, Johnny?"

"I'd like to come, but I have a paper to write for English," Johnny said. "Ginger knows the rock well. She can show you everything."

I wanted to hug him. Did he really have a paper to write or was he just being nice and giving me a chance to be alone with Scott? I didn't have a chance to decide, because the bell rang and Scott was already heading for the door.

"I'll meet you at the front gate, Ginger," he said. "I have a Jeep Explorer."

It figured.

5

I prayed that Ben and the entire football team—and Roni, Karen, Justine, and everyone else I knew—would be outside the building after school to watch me climb into Scott Masters's Jeep Explorer. But unfortunately, no one I knew was around as I came down the steps.

"Ginger, over here," Scott called, revving the engine of his Jeep. "Let's go."

I looked back hopefully, just in case Ben or Roni had appeared, but nobody was there. Still, not having an audience for my grand departure was only a small blemish on an otherwise perfect afternoon. It was one of those great fall days when the temperature finally begins to come down. The air was clear, the sky was a pure blue, and winter flowers were coming into bloom. We drove with the windows down and the warm, scented air in our faces. I began to wonder if I was dreaming. Was it really me sitting next to this gorgeous guy?

"I've dealt with Cromer and Ferndale before," he was saying, frowning as we drove into the setting sun. "They're tough, and they play dirty. We'll have to come up with something pretty darned good if we want to stop them."

"You think it's hopeless, then?" I asked in a small voice.

"I didn't say that," he answered, flashing me one of his wonderful smiles. "Personally, I enjoy a challenge. But we'll have to come up with something on Spirit Rock that will make them designate it as a nature preserve forever."

"We . . . uh . . . couldn't just take a rare plant from somewhere else and plant it in a little crevasse on Spirit Rock, could we?" I suggested.

He looked horrified. "Take a plant from somewhere else? You are kidding, right?"

"Of course. Just kidding," I said weakly. The guy had high principles as well as great looks!

He continued talking about fights he'd had with developers in the past. But the entire time I was thinking, *Do you have a girlfriend? Do you think I'm cute? Have you even noticed that I'm a girl?*

We parked in the dirt lot at the base of Spirit Rock. There was no sign of the developers, but there were more flags and stakes than last time. Scott frowned. "We're going to have to work fast on this," he said. "They're all ready to bring in the bulldozers. We'll get everybody on full alert at school tomorrow."

"Are you going to have us lie down in front of the bulldozers?" I asked. I meant it as a joke, but Scott didn't smile.

"We might," he said. "I hope it won't come to that."

Wait a minute, I thought. I'd seen that kind of thing on TV, but I never thought I'd have to do it personally. When I thought of lying on sharp rocks and cactus, waiting for a ten-ton bulldozer to run over me, I wondered how desperately I wanted to save Spirit Rock. Was I really cut out to save the planet?

Then I looked up at the familiar tumbled rocks of the summit and imagined a bulldozer scooping out a piece of my beautiful rock. I knew I was ready to lie down in front of it—especially if Scott Masters was there, too.

We set off around the base of the rock, following the little nature trail. Scott walked very fast, and I noticed that his hiking boots and thick socks protected his ankles from all the spiky, prickly things that were scratching me. I really would have to get new gear if I was going to be a serious environmentalist.

It took about half an hour to do a tour of the base. All the time I walked behind Scott, trying to think of witty, ecologically sound things to say. If only I knew something about plants! But I was scared that if I said, "Wait, what's that interesting flower?" he might reply, "That's a daisy," and I'd feel like the world's biggest fool. So I kept quiet and looked longingly at the back of his tanned neck. I was sweating by the time we got back, even though the evening breeze was cool.

"Nothing here, I'm afraid," Scott said. "If only there were some old saguaro cactus, we'd have it made." He turned and shielded his eyes to look at the summit. "Let's take a look up there," he said. "Is this the path?" Without waiting for an answer, he took off for the top.

I'd always thought I was in pretty good shape. Wrong. *Scott* was in good shape. *I* was gasping for air by the time we stood at the top. Now I had no breath for clever comments, even if I'd noticed a three-hundred-year-old saguaro growing by the path or a complete Native American altar among the rocks.

"Great view," he said. "You're right, Ginger. There's no way we can let them turn this into a resort. Pity there aren't any unusual plants. I guess we'll have to go the Indian route. If we can find anything to show that this was a regular worship site . . ."

"Johnny said it was sacred to his people for centuries."

"So are most of the hills around here," Scott said. "Unfortunately we'll need some proof." He was already heading back down again, stopping to turn over rocks as he went.

"What kind of proof?" I hurried to keep up with him.

"Archaeological evidence," Scott said.

"I used to find arrow . . . I mean projectile points up here," I said.

"You can find them all over," he said. "They don't prove anything. Some valuable pieces of pottery, especially with offerings still in them, would do it. A burial site would definitely do it."

"You mean we'd have to dig for bones?"

He nodded. "And we don't have much time. We have to talk to Johnny. Maybe he has contact with tribal elders. I know some people at the Museum of the American Indian. I bet they'd help. What we have to do is organize a giant dig in a hurry."

"Even if the land's already sold?"

"I don't think they can stop us from looking for artifacts before the bulldozers go in. Even Cromer and Ferndale wouldn't risk being insensitive to tribal history. They have to keep a good image."

We had reached the bottom again. Scott opened

the door of the Jeep for me. "Maybe this weekend," I suggested.

"If we can get it planned by then," he said. "I'll try to set up another meeting at school and let you know."

Scott started the Jeep and we drove off, leaving a plume of red dust behind us.

"I'm glad you brought me here, Ginger," he said as we drove down my street. "I'm always happy to know there are other people who care about the environment."

As we turned into the driveway, my heart lurched. Ben's truck was there, and Ben and Todd were just getting out of it. My timing couldn't have been more perfect. I couldn't wait to see Ben's face when he noticed Scott.

They looked up in surprise as I climbed out of the Jeep. "Bye, Scott. Thanks for driving me home," I called, very loudly. I was almost tempted to blow him a kiss.

Instead I waved and ran down the driveway like a cheerleader with a bouncy, cutesy run. "Hi, guys," I said sweetly to Ben and Todd. "Wasn't it nice of Scott to drive me home?"

"Where were you?" Todd asked. I tried not to look at Ben.

"Oh, Scott Masters and the ecology club are helping me with my campaign to save Spirit Rock," I said. "I found some people at school who really care about the same things I do." I paused long enough to let this sink in. Then I went on. "Especially Scott. He cares a lot. And I'm sure he'll be able to save Spirit Rock—he has so many great ideas. Besides, he's dealt with developers like this before. And he's great at getting media coverage. He's been on TV hundreds of times."

"Well, isn't that special?" Todd said. He and Ben grinned at each other.

"Ecology club!" Todd said, giving Ben a playful nudge as they walked into the house. "Talk about a bunch of dorks."

"Yeah, a bunch of dorks," Ben echoed with a phony laugh.

"If you two think that Scott Masters is a dork, you both need glasses," I said.

"Anyone who goes around protecting little flowers is a dork," Todd said. "You don't see football players wasting their energy on flowers and birds."

"Yeah," Ben agreed.

"That's right—you're all too busy wasting your energy on head butting," I said sweetly. "That's much more useful to society."

"I wish you'd give up this crazy idea, Ginger," Todd said. "You're just depriving Ben and me of great tips when we caddy for rich golf players."

"You'd probably let them flood the Grand Canyon so you could be a lifeguard," I snapped. "You are the most insensitive guys I've ever met. You don't care if the land around you is wrecked. You don't care about people's feelings. You don't care about anything."

I looked directly at Ben. I wanted him to say, "Not me. I care what you're doing, Ginger. I care about you." But his face was like a mask, with no expression on it. I couldn't even tell whether he was jealous or not. Maybe he hadn't noticed that Scott Masters was a babe. Maybe he was even relieved that I'd met Scott Masters, so that he could break up with me gently. Well, if that's the way he wanted it, I'd show him! Who would want Ben when they could have Scott Masters?

The next morning my alarm woke me to total darkness. For a moment I lay there, my heart pounding, wondering what was happening. Then I remembered—I had to get my hair washed and styled, my makeup on, and my outfit perfect before I went to school.

Todd hammered on the bathroom door several times. "Ginger, what are you doing, for pete's sake? Ginger—have you gone back to sleep? Have you died? GINGER! I need to get in there. You're making me late."

I didn't care. Let him find out what other girls were like every morning. Maybe he and his creepy friend Ben would finally realize that I was a young woman who mattered.

I blow-dried my hair so it was soft and fluffy, then I put it into a bouncy ponytail. I figured that Scott, being the outdoor type, wouldn't go for fussy clothes and lots of makeup. I even convinced myself that he wouldn't think my freckles were too terrible. I used just enough eyeliner to highlight my eyes, a little mascara to give me long, sweeping lashes, and then loads of blush for that glowing, healthy look. The result wasn't bad. Then I selected a natural cotton shirt, which I tied at my midriff, and my shortest pair of white shorts to show off my long, athletic legs.

I sound like Justine, I thought in horror. But I had to admit that I looked better than usual. Todd would probably laugh, but maybe Scott would notice that I looked like a girl today—healthy, outdoorsy, ecology minded, and definitely female.

"Wow! What's the big occasion?" Roni asked as I got on the bus.

"Not what—*who,*" I said.

"What do you mean?"

"If you want to know, I've met a gorgeous guy," I

told her. "Incredibly cute. Drop-dead gorgeous. I plan to make him notice me."

"Tell me more!" Roni said.

"Well, I went to the ecology club meeting—"

"Don't tell me you found a babe at the ecology club," she interrupted. "I was sure they'd all be dorky."

"This one isn't," I said. "He is a Greek god."

"I'll have to see for myself," she said. "When does your ecology club meet again?"

"Scott's trying to arrange another meeting as soon as possible so that we can start digging for Native American artifacts," I said.

Roni looked at me skeptically. "You're beginning to talk like them," she said. "Are you sure they haven't brainwashed you? Maybe in reality this guy is only five foot one and covered with zits."

"You wait until you see him," I said. "Come with me when I go to the ecology club meeting."

"Only as far as the door," she said. "I don't want to find myself signed up to hunt for bugs."

I didn't say anything else. I just sat there with a smug smile on my face. I was dying to see how Roni reacted when she saw Scott. Knowing Roni, she'd probably be offering to throw herself in front of the bulldozers to impress him!

"Let me make one thing very clear," I said. "I saw him first."

“And you think he’s the one to make Ben jealous?”

“Ben who?” I asked innocently. Roni raised her eyebrows. “Just kidding,” I said. “But a guy like this could easily take my mind off Ben, if Ben really is planning to dump me. In fact, I think I could survive very well dating a guy like Scott.”

But even as I said it, I felt my stomach do a flip. How could I make a joke about losing Ben—the first guy who had ever mattered to me? Knowing that he didn’t care about me wasn’t funny. It was the worst feeling I’d ever had.

6

The morning announcements said that the ecology club would be meeting again at lunchtime for an emergency session. All members were urged to attend, as action was needed on a vital issue. Scott certainly didn't waste time. *What a go-getter,* I thought. A man of action, a man of principles. I liked that.

I ate lunch quickly with my friends and then I got up, brushing the crumbs off my lap. "See you later, guys. I have to go save Spirit Rock," I said.

Roni, Karen, and Justine all got to their feet. "Are you kidding?" Justine said. "You've done nothing but blab about Alta Mesa's answer to Luke Perry all morning. We want to take a peek at this gorgeous guy. We'll escort you to the meeting."

"Well, okay," I said hesitantly, "but don't you dare say anything to embarrass me." I wasn't sure that I wanted to make my entrance with three friends giggling at the door. That was the kind of thing little freshmen did, and Scott was a mature senior.

"As if we would," Justine said, looking hurt. "Of course, I can only speak for myself. Roni and Karen might act childishly, but I am always mature and cool around strange guys—" She paused to let out a piercing scream. "Eek! No! Run for your lives!"

"Justine, what is it?" We crowded around her as she flapped her arms hysterically, trying to drag us away.

"Look over there! It's the nerds. Quick. Hide before it's too late!"

We looked around, but there was no convenient girls' bathroom or open door to dodge into. Besides, they had seen us.

"Yoo-hoo, girls!" Owen called in his squeaky voice. He was the shrimpy one, the head nerd. He broke into a robotlike run.

"We've been looking for you all over," Ronald said, peering at us intensely through his thick glasses. "You weren't in your usual lunch spot, so we thought that maybe you were trying to find us."

"In your dreams," Justine muttered.

"I'd rather look for an invasion of killer bees," Karen whispered to me.

"What do you want us for?" Roni demanded.

"Walter's new computer program," Owen said proudly. "Go on, tell them, Walter."

Walter, the computer nerd, was painfully shy. He turned bright red and swallowed hard. "I perfected my personality assessment program," he said. "You answer a bunch of questions and it tells you what kind of personality you have."

"We already know our personalities, stupid," Justine said. "I'm friendly, cool, and outgoing. Roni is loud. Karen is a little too quiet and shy. Ginger is a tomboy—"

"And Justine is known for her tact," Karen finished for her. We laughed and Justine flushed.

"Anyway, this program will probably work about as well as your last pathetic attempt," Justine said hastily. "You remember your dating program? You couldn't come up with a match for me in the entire school!"

"That was because you wanted someone rich, intelligent, and athletic who drove an expensive car and looked gorgeous," Roni said, laughing. "Such a guy doesn't exist."

Yes, he does, I thought. *His name's Scott Masters, and Justine won't get a chance with him.*

"I'm sorry that I won't be able to discover my personality right now," I said, "but I have to get to the ecology club meeting."

"I didn't know you were into ecology," Owen said.

"Maybe she's saving up for something special," Wolfgang said in his deep, rumbly voice. He was very large and wore the most terrible sweaters in clashing colors. Today he wasn't wearing his usual purple-and-brown stag, but a sweater we hadn't seen before: an abstract design in yellow, red, and black. At least there was hope that his wardrobe was expanding.

"She's what?" Ronald asked.

"She's starting a savings account. That's a good idea," Wolfgang said seriously.

Walter started laughing—a horrible *hee-snort, hee-snort*. "That's economy, not ecology," he said.

"So what's ecology?" Wolfgang asked.

"Saving endangered species. That kind of thing."

"Oh," Wolfgang said. From his expression he probably didn't know what endangered species were, but he wasn't about to ask.

"Ginger's trying to save Spirit Rock from developers," Roni said.

"So that still leaves the rest of you," Walter said with a creepy smile. "You guys can come down to the computer lab and have your personality tests run, can't you?"

"Uh, no, we can't," Roni said quickly.

"Why not?"

"Because . . . because we're also going to sign

up to work on Spirit Rock," Karen said.

"We are?" Justine asked loudly. "We're going to look for old Indian bones? I really don't think—"

Roni must have kicked her, because Justine yelped and shut up. "Remember how we agreed to support Ginger, Justine?" Roni asked pointedly.

"No, I thought—" she began, but Karen swung her around and gazed earnestly into her face.

"Remember, Justine, how we decided we ought to go to the ecology club meeting today?"

"Oh, yeah." Justine nodded as she finally grasped what Roni was getting at. "Now I remember. Of course. We have to support Ginger. Spirit Rock is very important. Sorry, guys. Have to rush to the ecology club now."

She grabbed my arm and started to propel me down the hall.

After a while I looked back. "I don't want to alarm you guys," I said, "but the nerds are still following us."

Roni glanced back. "Oh, gross," she said. "You don't think they're coming to the ecology club, too, do you?"

My worst nightmare began to take shape. I had gotten up at dawn just to make myself look good. All I wanted was for Scott to notice me. Well, he'd notice me all right—especially if I entered the room with three giggling friends and four nerds in tow. "This can't be happening," I said desperately. "We have to do something."

Immediately Justine spun around. "Where do you guys think you're going?" she demanded.

Four terrified faces looked back at her. "To the computer lab," Ronald squeaked.

"Rats," Karen said. "The computer lab is at the end of the same hall we're going to."

"Now we really are stuck helping Ginger with the ecology club," Justine said with a big sigh.

"Of course we are," Roni told her. "We said we would."

"I thought we were just saying that to the nerds," Justine said. "I didn't think we were really committing ourselves to digging up dead people."

"You don't have to if you don't want to, Justine," I said, laughing at her expression. "Scott is hoping to get in experts from the Museum of the American Indian. They probably won't even let us do any digging. We might do more harm than good."

"Oh. Okay, then," Justine said. "I think I'd freak out if I saw a skull staring up at me."

"Me too," Karen agreed, and Roni nodded.

"Look, guys," I said. "You really don't have to do this. I understand."

"Well . . . I do have stuff to do this weekend," Roni said. "I'd like to help, but . . ."

"Me too," Karen said. "I promised James I'd go over to his house . . ."

"And I have to help my stepmother choose stuff for the nursery," Justine said. "I want to make sure my new little sister or brother comes into the world with the right designer labels."

We looked at each other and giggled. I wondered if Justine's new brother or sister would instinctively know a blanket was designed by Calvin Klein. Maybe people like Justine really were born that way.

"It's okay," I said. "I really didn't expect any of you to come to the dig. They probably don't want too many people crowding the site." Secretly I was a little relieved they weren't coming. I didn't want my friends hanging around while I tried to impress Scott. What if he liked one of them better than me?

Besides, saving Spirit Rock had become *my* thing. I wanted it to be *only* mine . . . and Scott's.

We reached the door of the classroom. I opened it and glanced around. Scott was sitting on a desk near the window with his back to us. I nudged Roni. "That's him!" I whispered.

"I can't see him," Roni whispered back.

Out loud I said, "Well, bye, guys, see you by the lockers before math."

As I'd hoped, my voice was loud enough to make Scott turn toward the door. His face broke into a dazzling smile. "Oh, hi, Ginger. Glad you could make it," he said. "I think I've managed to set things in motion with the museum."

I closed the door on my friends and hurried to join the group sitting around Scott. I was amazed at what he had managed to do in a few short hours. He'd arranged for the experts at the museum to come out this weekend, and he'd spoken to someone at Cromer and Ferndale about allowing us one last inspection of the hill before it became a hotel. They thought we were just a bunch of kids looking for arrowheads. Little did they know!

I was feeling really hopeful by the end of lunch hour. I had a whole weekend with Scott to look forward to, but it was more than that. Until that moment I'd always felt like a kid. Adults ran the world and made decisions for me, and I had to go along with them. Now I felt that I had my destiny in my own hands. I really could make a difference and change the world. The other members of the ecology club talked excitedly about what we might find. All the time they were talking, I kept thinking, *I was the one who started this.* I practically floated out of the classroom when the meeting was over.

My friends were waiting for me at our lockers.

"That was really nice of you, Ginger," Roni said as I came down the hall.

"Yeah, thanks a lot," Justine added.

"She didn't mean to do it, guys," Karen said kindly.

"Didn't mean to do what?" I asked.

"You slammed the door in our faces just as the nerds came around the corner," Justine said. "They tried to drag us to their computer lab and make us take their creepy personality test."

"You know what they're like, Ginger," Karen added. "They just won't take no for an answer. We tried to be nice and give them the brush-off in the nicest way—"

"Except me," Justine said. "I wanted to tell them to go back to their swamp and leave us alone."

"But we wouldn't let her," Roni finished. "They can't help being social outcasts."

"So did you manage to escape?" I asked.

Roni grinned. "I had to pretend to feel sick," she said. "I threatened to throw up on them and they ran for cover. They couldn't get away fast enough."

I laughed. "That one worked well in grade school, too. I'm sorry I left you in the hall. My mind just went blank when Scott smiled at me." I looked from one face to the next. "So, what do you think? Is he adorable or what?"

"Oh, sure. He's gorgeous," Karen said, but she gave Roni a funny look.

"And we're going to be working together all

weekend," I went on. "All alone among the rocks . . . Don't you think Ben will be wild with jealousy? And if he's not, maybe I'd rather have Scott as a boyfriend. Who wouldn't?"

"Ginger," Roni said. "You might have mentioned that the guy you had a crush on was Scott Masters."

"Why?"

"Ginger—Scott Masters," Roni said, shaking her head as if I were dumb. "Only the most overachieving senior in the school! Senior council, debate team, Harvard and Yale fighting to give him scholarships. I don't think he's going to be interested in a freshman."

"You said yourself that lots of upperclassmen date younger people."

"Yeah, but this guy can have his pick. How many guys do you know who are smart, athletic, and gorgeous?" she went on.

"Maybe something will click this weekend, when we're working together," I said.

"Oh, please," Justine said, grinning. "Believe me, if I thought a freshman had any chance with him, I'd get interested in ecology myself. I'd even risk getting dirt under my fingernails. But if I wouldn't stand a chance, you certainly wouldn't. I mean, you don't even own any designer shorts."

"I don't think Scott is the kind of guy who cares

about designer shorts, Justine," I said. "Ours would be a meeting of the minds."

"Oh, yeah?" Roni said, giving me a playful nudge. "If all you're interested in is a great mind, I'm sure Walter the nerd has one."

"Okay, so I admit that his great body does have something to do with it," I said. "But I'm sure he's not the type who cares too much about looks. He likes healthy, outdoor types, just like me. And I'm counting on you guys."

"For what?" Justine asked.

"This is a job for the Boyfriend Club," I said. "It's our biggest challenge yet. You have between now and this weekend to think of ways for me to impress Scott."

I saw the look my friends exchanged. "Come on, Ginger," Roni said at last. "You're not serious, are you?"

"Sure I am," I said. "I've never been more serious in my life. I want to get Scott interested in me. I would die for a chance to go out with him. After all, wasn't this why we set up the Boyfriend Club in the first place?"

"To help us get dates, sure," Karen said. "But you already have Ben. We helped you get together with him."

"And now I'm about to lose him," I said. "This is a surefire way to get him back. If I start hanging out with Scott, I know Ben will get jealous and come running back to me." I stopped and looked from one face to the next. "So how about it, guys? Can I count on you? This really means a lot to me."

Justine coughed nervously. "What exactly do you think we can do, Ginger?"

"The sort of things we've done to meet other boys."

"Our plans never went exactly as we expected," Roni reminded me. "Remember when we tried to set Karen up with that musician guy? Remember Justine and that wild biker? Total disasters."

"But four heads are better than one," I said. "I need ideas."

"We gave you a makeover when you wanted Ben to think of you as more grown up," Justine said.

"But that wouldn't work with Scott," I said. "I told you, I'm sure he wouldn't notice if I wore the most expensive clothes in the world. I need to impress him in a way he'll think is important."

"You'd better lie down in front of that bulldozer, then," Karen said.

"I'm prepared to do that, if necessary," I said seriously, "but so are all the other ecology club members. We take our planet saving very seriously. What I need is something that nobody else can do."

"Like what?" Roni demanded.

I shrugged hopelessly. "I have no idea," I said.

7

As the weekend approached, I had to admit to myself that I didn't stand much chance of getting Scott's attention. I've never seen anyone more totally focused. He was so wrapped up in planning the dig that he wouldn't have noticed if King Kong handed him the map he asked for. I would have to do something absolutely incredible to get his mind off Spirit Rock and onto me.

Maybe if I came into the room and said, "Guess what, Scott, I just won the Nobel Peace Prize" or "Hey, Scott, want to come with me to meet the President this afternoon?" he would notice I was alive. But somehow I didn't think he'd believe either of those things.

I finally persuaded my friends that it was up to the Boyfriend Club to help me. After a lot of stalling, they promised they would try to come up with something to make me stand out from the crowd. I knew they were right—this was really out of their league. I mean, Justine was great at lending people expensive clothes, and Roni and Karen were good at snooping out details about a boy, but none of those would work in my case. I had already met Scott, and I don't think he would have looked up from his planning if I'd walked across the room in a designer evening gown. Also, the whole school knew every detail of his life. After all, he appeared on the front page of the school newspaper often enough.

I had browsed through old copies of the newspaper in the school library. "Scott Masters to represent city in state debating tournament." "Scott Masters meets President during Washington trip." There was even a photo of Scott shaking Charles Barclay's hand at a charity basketball game. The guy did everything, went everywhere. The only thing the photos didn't show was a girlfriend. Roni's rumor machine thought that he was dating a girl from a private school, which gave me hope. At least that meant he had time in his busy schedule for a girl. In which case, there was no reason why that girl couldn't be me!

When I came home from school on Thursday evening, after a final planning session with the ecology club, I found Todd and Ben in the kitchen, making chili.

"Hey, save some for me," I said, watching a large pot of chili disappear into two bowls. "I'm starving."

"Sorry, kid, but we've been working out," Todd said. "It was weights day at football practice. We need energy."

"And I don't?" I demanded. "I've been busy, too, you know. This Spirit Rock business is taking a lot of effort."

The guys grinned at each other. "Oh, sure," Todd said. "Are you doing special weight training so you can lift your magnifying glass and your wildflower book?"

"That's all you know," I said. "We're planning a full-scale dig on the rock all weekend. We're hoping to discover a Native American worship site."

"You're going to be digging up there all weekend?" Ben asked.

"You bet."

"Oh," he said. "Does that mean you won't be coming to the game on Saturday? We've got that big tournament in Glendale. I thought you were going to come."

"Why, are you planning to put me in as quarterback if you're losing?" I asked with a grin. "I mean, it won't make any difference if I'm there or not, will it?"

Ben shrugged. "I guess not," he said. "I just thought that . . . It's okay, forget it. The dig's more important to you."

"The dig's very important," I said. "And I don't see why it matters to you if I'm at your football game or not. It's not as if you ever talk to me when you're with your football buddies."

"But I like to know you're there," he said, looking like a lost little boy.

"What a totally sexist reaction," I snapped. "You just want a woman to be like an ornament or something. You like to know I'm there, but it's beneath your dignity to talk to me."

"Hey, it's not like that," Ben said, and his voice had a sharp edge to it. "It's just that we're supposed to stay focused."

"Yeah, the coach would give us a hard time if he saw us talking to a girl," Todd agreed. "Especially a girl like you. He wouldn't trust Ben's judgment if he saw his taste in women."

I said, "Shut up, Todd," at the same time that Ben said, "Come on, Todd. Give her a break." Todd made a face and turned back to his chili.

Ben looked at me. "What I was trying to say, Ginger, was that it's hard enough for me and Todd to get any playing time as it is, being new. We don't want to blow it. And the coach almost promised he'd try me at wide receiver this week."

"Well, I'm sorry," I said, "but I have to be at the dig. Scott and I have it all planned."

"Scott Masters?" Ben asked.

"Of course," I said. "You knew he was the one organizing this, didn't you? He is absolutely incredible. You should see how he manages to get things settled. He only has to pick up a phone and whatever he needs is done instantly."

"Well, isn't that nice. Scott Masters—what a guy!" Todd said, smirking at Ben. I didn't notice Ben smiling back. *Maybe, just maybe,* I thought, *this is starting to work after all.*

I went into my bedroom, already imagining Scott and myself digging up the most amazing stuff. We'd save the rock forever and become famous. I wandered around my room while my mind was miles away with Scott.

But at the back of my mind, a nagging thought was cutting into my fantasy. There was something different about my room! At first I couldn't decide what it was. Then I got to the part in the fantasy about digging up the Native American goodies, and suddenly, I knew. My display of arrowheads was missing from my wall!

I looked all around the room, wondering if I had taken it down to show my friends, but it was nowhere.

I stormed out again, catching the guys with mouthfuls of chili. "Okay, wise guys," I said. "Where did you hide them?"

"What are you talking about?" Todd asked. "Have you finally flipped?"

"You know what I'm talking about!" I yelled. "My arrowheads. They're gone, and no one else could have taken them. Where are they?"

"Why would Todd and I take your arrowheads?" Ben demanded.

"Maybe you weren't in on this, Ben, because you usually are more mature than my stupid brother," I said, "but it figures, doesn't it? I start talking about saving Spirit Rock and you don't want it saved. You're scared I'll show my arrowheads to someone as proof that it's a Native American site."

"Baloney!" Todd said. "Why would we care what you or your dumb arrowheads do?"

"Because you hid my G.I. Joe collection."

"Give me a break, Ginger. I'm not ten years old anymore," he said. "I've got better things to do with my life now."

"Okay, I believe you," I said. My brother is a rotten liar. I'd know if he was lying. "But it's still weird. I know the arrowheads were there last week, because I showed them to Roni and Karen and Justine. Things don't just disappear."

"Are you sure you didn't take them for show-and-tell to Scott?" Ben asked sweetly.

"I mentioned them to Scott," I said. "But he said that projectile points are too common to be impressive. So where could they have gone?"

"Don't ask us," Todd said.

"I liked those arrowheads," I said. I had a horrible feeling I might do something really embarrassing like cry. "They were special to me when I was a little kid. I'd hate to lose them now."

Ben got to his feet. "Okay," he said. "We really don't have much time, but we'll help you look if they're that special to you."

His being nice made me feel even worse. "That's the trouble," I sniffled. "I don't know where to look. I've been through my room."

"Maybe they got carried out to the garage. Maybe your dad took them to show to somebody . . ."

"I don't think so," I said. "He always used to ask me why I wanted to bring all that dirty old stuff into the house."

"We can do a quick check of the garage, anyway," Ben said. "Come on, Todd. Get off your duff and help."

Todd got to his feet. "This is a lot of fuss about a few pieces of rock," he said. "I bet they weren't even real arrowheads, just chips of rock she found when she was a little kid."

We went through the living room and kitchen really quickly. Todd's bedroom turned up nothing. Then we did a quick check of the garage.

"You see," I said. "They're not here—"

Todd let out a roar of anger. "Hey, what happened to my dinosaur bones?"

"Your what?" Ben asked.

Todd glared at us. "Remember I found those bones when we were camping? I was sure they were dinosaur bones, even though Dad said they weren't. But I brought them home and I kept them in a box, right here next to the Christmas decorations. The box is gone."

"Do you think Dad cleaned the garage and threw them out without telling us?" I asked, worried.

Todd shook his head. "Why would he have left all this other junk? Look at it—empty shoe boxes, the carburetor from his old truck, a bent bike wheel. There's heaps of junk in this garage. He wouldn't just have chosen one box of bones and one collection of arrowheads."

"You're right," said Ben.

"It's the developers," I gasped. "How could I not realize it? They've been going through the neighborhood, taking out any evidence of Indians so that we can't prove the Pima were ever here."

Todd and Ben laughed. "Oh, sure," Todd said. "A

mega-corporation sends spies to the Hartmans' house to steal Ginger's valuable collection of arrowheads and Todd's bones. I can just see it."

"I guess not," I said, smiling too.

"I'm sure they'll show up," Ben said gently.

"I hope so." I sighed. "I'll be so upset if they're gone. Especially now that I'll never be able to look for any more."

I glanced out the window. The sun was going down and Spirit Rock looked beautiful. I just couldn't picture it covered with stores and shoppers.

"I'm going to jog up Spirit Rock right now," I said. "It might be my last chance."

I sprinted across the field until I reached the wilderness area at the bottom of the rock. Nothing had been done since the stakes went in. I kept expecting to see bulldozers and other earthmovers, but they hadn't come yet. It was just me and the rock, the way it had always been.

As I began to climb, I felt my tension slip away. The magic of the rock was still working. Up and up I went, not slowing at all, until the blood was pounding in my head and my side hurt when I breathed. I could hear the wind whispering through cracks in the rocks. I had sometimes heard voices in that wind when I had come here. I heard them again now, soft whispers that seemed to have words in them. I stopped, entranced. Maybe the rock was trying to communicate with me. Maybe the spirits of old were crying out to me, asking me to help them save the rock.

Then one voice spoke, clearer than the others. It said: "Watch what you're doing, Roni. You almost made me chip a fingernail."

I froze. The voice was very like Justine's. I looked up into the wild tumble of rock and scrub on the slope above me. I thought I could make out movement in a patch of deep shadow, but it could have been a trick of the light. I began to wonder if the rock spirits were playing jokes on me. Why would Justine be up on the rock, hiding in the shrubs? Why would Justine be here at all? She had made it very clear that the rock wasn't her favorite place. Cautiously, in case the voices did turn out to be something supernatural, I began to pick my way through the rocks and bushes.

"Is this where the leg bone would go on a dead body?" asked Roni's voice, loud and clear.

I ran to my friends. "What do you think you're doing?" I demanded. All three of them leaped to their feet, nearly falling over in their fright.

"Ginger! You scared the daylights out of me!" Karen gasped.

"You were spying on us!" Roni said.

"I could've fallen over the edge," Justine said. "You shouldn't have snuck up on us like that."

"I wasn't spying on you. I went jogging up the rock because I was upset. I didn't know you were here until I heard Justine's voice."

"See, Justine. We told you to keep your voice down in case somebody came," Karen said.

"How was I supposed to know that Ginger would show up!" Justine said.

"It could just as easily have been one of the contractor's men and we wouldn't have wanted them to see us," Roni commented.

I looked from their guilty faces to the hole in the ground. "What exactly were you doing up here?" I asked. Then I took a closer look at the ground. "My arrowheads!" I exclaimed. "And Todd's bones."

My friends looked even more guilty now. "We were just trying to help," Karen said in a small voice.

"By hiding my arrowheads?"

"You kept on and on about helping you with Scott," Roni said, throwing up her chin defiantly the way she always did when she was caught doing something bad. "So we came up with this idea."

"We knew how much saving Spirit Rock meant to you," Karen said, "and this seemed like the only way to save it."

"I must be dumb. I still don't get it," I said.

"It's simple." Justine waved her arms in a grand gesture. "It's brilliant. A stroke of genius. Of course, I was the one who came up with it. You said that the only way to save this place is to unearth an old Indian site, right? And you also want to make a big impression with Scott. So, we kill two birds with one stone."

"What she's trying to say," Karen interpreted, "is that we were going to bury stuff to make it look like an Indian grave. And then you were going to find it and the rock would be saved and Scott would think you were a hero."

I looked down at the bizarre collection lying in the open trench: Todd's bones, which were almost certainly from a dead cow, now arranged like a weird skeleton; my arrowheads; beads from an old headdress Roni used to wear when we played dress-up; bits of broken flowerpot; and a few feathers. I started to laugh. I laughed until I felt tears running down my cheeks.

"We were only trying to help," Roni said.

I knelt and picked up a piece of broken pottery. "This says 'Made in Japan,'" I managed to say between giggles.

"So? The Native Americans were great traders. Maybe they traded arrowheads for teacups," Karen said, but she was starting to laugh, too.

"You guys," I gasped, fighting for breath. "This is absolutely the sweetest thing that anyone has ever done for me. Unfortunately, it's also the dumbest. There is no way it could work."

"It might," Roni said defiantly. "It might just work."

8

"It might just work," Roni repeated for the zillionth time on Saturday morning. She had stopped by to wish me luck on her way to go Rollerblading with Drew and his friends.

"It won't work. It can't possibly work," I insisted. "I don't know why I let you guys talk me into leaving the stuff up there."

"Because you'll do anything to impress Scott," Roni said with a knowing grin. "And speaking of impressing guys, I hope Drew won't think I look like a wimp." She held up her arms and legs to show me her kneepads, elbow pads, and wrist guards.

I grinned. "You look like a warrior princess from a video game with all that armor on," I said.

Roni made a face. "The guy insisted that I needed to wear all this stuff when I rented the skates," she said. "I guess it makes sense, since I've never tried Rollerblading before."

"At least you won't break anything if you fall down," I said. "Are you sure you don't want to borrow a pillow for your tush?"

"Very funny. I'm not even sure I want to go." She frowned.

"You'll be fine. You've tried ice-skating, and I hear it's exactly the same," I comforted.

"Yeah, but you can dig your blades into the ice to stop. I have no idea how to stop these things. If I don't come back, I'm heading for California, hoping to bump into something before I reach the Pacific Ocean."

"If you're so worried, then don't go."

She looked amazed. "Are you kidding? Miss out on a day with Drew in the park? I just hope he and his friends don't skate too fast for me. Wish me luck."

"Good luck," I said, "and wish me luck with Scott and the dig."

"You don't need luck. You've got a custom-made grave site waiting for you," she said, giving me a wave as she headed back to her house. "Complete with rare Japanese-Indian pottery!" she yelled over her shoulder.

I wished I had her confidence. Now, in the cold light of morning, I didn't see how the collection of bones and broken china could fool anybody for a minute. How could I have agreed to leave it there? How could my friends have believed it looked like the real thing?

I had tried to make them see that they were just making fools of themselves, and me, by leaving the bones and arrowheads there, but they had begged me to give it a chance.

"What have you got to lose?" Justine demanded. "If nobody else has found anything all day and you unearth our things, you'll still be a hero for a while. It will take time before they find out it's not a genuine site."

"Maybe the newspapers will have reporters up there and they'll take your picture," Karen added. "You'll be a star and Scott will think you're smart and wonderful."

"Until the whole world discovers that I'm a phony. Then Scott won't want anything to do with me."

"It might just work," Roni said again. "I've got a good feeling about this . . ."

I didn't. Now as I crossed the field in the slanting sunlight, I wondered how I had ever let them talk me into leaving the dumb stuff up there. If Karen hadn't painted such a wonderful picture of my instant fame,

I'd probably have carried the bones and arrowheads back to the house where they belonged. Knowing they were up there now, in a shallow grave between the rocks, made me break out into a cold sweat. *As soon as I get there, I'm going to remove them,* I decided. Most people weren't arriving for the dig until nine. I would be up there at eight-thirty.

Spirit Rock was deserted as I ran through the scrub and started to climb. Today I wasn't conscious of the beauty or the magic or the wind blowing in my hair. I was still clammy all over with embarrassment. I kept imagining the guy from the museum turning over the Japanese cup in his hand. "Someone's been playing a trick on you, young lady," he'd say, and everyone would laugh, including Scott. "How could you have been so easily fooled, Ginger?" Scott would ask. "An idiot could tell that this stuff is not Native American."

As I climbed higher, I realized something awful. It wasn't going to be as easy as I thought to find the place where the junk was buried. Every twist and turn in the path produced an area of rock and stunted bushes that looked horribly like the one before. Why hadn't I taken the trouble to look for distinguishing marks on rocks, unusually twisted bushes—anything that would let me find my site in a hurry? It had all been so obvious when I was up there with my friends.

I was sure that the great big gash of earth they had dug up would stand out like an open wound. But it didn't.

I climbed and climbed, until I realized that I must have come too far. This was the summit area and all rock, no earth for grave sites. *Think!* I commanded myself. I remembered that there had been one big paloverde bush, because Justine had hung her jacket on it. And there must have been footprints! Not too many people left the trail, so I'd just have to look for footprints heading into the rocks. I wondered if Justine had been wearing her Italian sandals. They would make an easy print to follow!

I began to feel like a genuine Native American scout as I came down the trail, studying the marks in the dust. It didn't take me long to realize that I would have made a terrible scout. I couldn't find any footprints leaving the trail at all. Where the ground wasn't hard and rocky, it was covered with small plants, and I couldn't tell if any of them had been crushed underfoot recently.

I tried several places I thought looked familiar, but there was no sign of recent feet. Then, at last, I saw what I had been looking for: Justine's heel print among the spiky plants. Time was running short. Any minute now the others would arrive. I clambered over rocks until I saw the bush Justine's jacket had hung on. I heaved a big sigh of relief as I knelt down to dig.

It wasn't easy to identify the exact grave my friends had dug: the whole area had been trampled, and they had even attempted to put plants back in place. I dug frantically. I couldn't believe they had buried the arrowheads so deep. But at last I was rewarded: a string of dirty beads came to the surface. It was amazing how quickly they could become old looking, I thought. They had looked bright, plastic, and phony when Roni put them in. But there was no time to think about that now. I kept digging. Almost immediately, I found a bone.

Great, I thought. *Now if I can just dig up the rest of this stupid stuff before anyone comes . . .*

It was too late. I hadn't heard anyone coming up the path, but suddenly a voice said, "Ginger! You got here early. We were supposed to meet for orientation at nine." I looked up to see Johnny standing there, looking very Native American in his fringed jacket against the backdrop of red rocks.

He grinned as he glanced over his shoulder. "Dr. Delgado from the museum is probably going to be mad that you started without him. He's taking this very seriously. He gave us this long spiel about treating the site with extreme delicacy and how archaeologists sometimes have to brush away sand one grain at a time. . . ."

As he was speaking, his gaze went down to the large patch of dug-up earth beside me. There was no escape.

"I can understand why you wanted to get started," he said kindly. "I know how important it is to you to find something that's historically valuable. I feel the same way. Even more so because it's my ancestors we're talking about." He perched on the boulder beside me.

"Just imagine, Ginger, if we did find a worship site the Pima used hundreds of years ago. I'm so excited. I just wish I knew where to get started. There's a lot of rock to dig over in one weekend. I can't see that we have much chance—" He broke off as he saw what I was trying to conceal in the earth. "Wait! Is that a bone you've got there?"

"This? Oh, this is nothing," I said, my face turning bright scarlet. I couldn't explain to him, a real Native American, that my crazy friends had invented a phony Pima grave.

He came to squat beside me. "Let me see," he said excitedly.

"It's nothing, Johnny . . ."

"Did you find it right here? How did you know to start digging here?"

Before I could stop him, he took the bone from me. "This looks old," he said.

"It's just an animal bone. Some old buck probably died here," I said.

"And beads!" he exclaimed as he noticed them lying beside me. "You've found beads! We've got to get Dr. Delgado."

"No, wait, Johnny, you don't understand! It's not really—" But he was already leaping across the rocks.

"Dr. Delgado!" he yelled. "Up here! We've found something!"

I looked around wildly. The only way down was the way Dr. Delgado and everyone else was now coming up. I wouldn't have time to dig up the rest of the stuff. I'd just have to bluff my way out.

Think up a good story, Ginger! I commanded myself, but my brain wouldn't cooperate. *Let's see, I was coming up the path and I noticed the bone sticking out of the soil? I've been up here before and found a bone once? I was pretty sure it was an animal bone, but I thought I'd just double-check before anyone got here. I didn't want anyone else to get their hopes up and be disappointed.* Yeah, that sounded good. It also didn't make me sound like too much of an idiot in front of Scott.

Footsteps were coming up the path now. I could hear the buzz of excited chatter. I tried to get my story straight in my head. I scrambled to my feet, convinced I must look totally guilty, as a group came up the trail, led by a distinguished-looking gray-haired man with a big, bushy mustache. In his hand he clutched my bone. Scott was right behind him.

"This is the young lady?" I heard him ask Johnny. Without waiting for an answer, he left the trail and clambered across the rocks to join me. "How do you do? I'm Dr. Delgado. I understand you've already made a significant discovery here."

"Not really," I stammered. "You see . . . I remembered seeing—I mean, I come up here a lot and I thought . . . I, um, I didn't want anyone to think they'd found something when it was just animal bones."

I'm sure I wasn't making much sense to anyone. I wasn't even making much sense to me.

"What made you select this particular site to begin digging?" Dr. Delgado asked. "Was it pure luck, or had you been doing fieldwork up here before?"

Scott leaned forward and smiled down at me. "Ginger probably knows the rock better than anyone else," he said. "She's been coming up here all her life."

"Then it is only right that she should make the first discovery," Dr. Delgado said, beaming at me.

I swallowed hard. Should I tell them now? Should I come right out and say that I was a phony? That the bone he held in his hand had belonged to a cow and then to my brother? That the beads on the ground were from the five-and-dime store and that if we kept on digging, we'd soon come up with a Japanese cup? I knew I had to tell them. It wasn't fair to see their excited, hopeful faces all smiling at me. I felt like the world's biggest fake.

"Dr. Delgado, I'm afraid you're going to be disappointed," I managed to say. "You see, this isn't anything at all. It's just an old animal bone and—"

"On the contrary, young lady. I'm almost certain that this is a human femur," he said. "And if I'm not mistaken, it's of considerable age. Of course, we'll have to send it to the university for carbon dating. . . ."

I was staring at him, openmouthed. Could it be possible that my brother had actually had human bones in that box all these years? But even if it was a human bone, I'd still have to tell the truth: that it was only buried here yesterday. I knew that finding it here would save Spirit Rock, and I wanted that more than anything in the world. But when it came down to it, I couldn't let Spirit Rock be saved by a lie. The spirits of the rock wouldn't want that.

"I have a confession to make, Dr. Delgado," I said quietly.

"I can see. I can see," he said gleefully. "You're frightened I'm going to be angry because you started digging without us—and in such an amateur fashion, too. Why, look at these beads: we're lucky you didn't smash them with your reckless digging, considering their age. . . ." He picked them up. I held my breath, waiting for him to drop them in disgust, exclaiming, "But these are only plastic!"

But he didn't. He held them lovingly in his hand. "Perfect examples of fourteenth-century Indian art," he whispered. "We must proceed very cautiously with the rest of this site. I rather think that we are going to find some real treasures today."

With that, he banished everybody except for his two assistants. They immediately began working with sifting boxes and brushes as Dr. Delgado tenderly dug through the earth. I stood a few feet away, feeling very confused. I didn't know what to think. Was this guy a phony who didn't know the difference between plastic beads and fourteenth-century Indian art? I waited to hear what he'd say when he got to the Japanese teacup. But before he could dig that up, he gave a deep sigh, which was echoed by his assistants. Out of the ground came this perfect little basket.

It was woven in a complicated chevron pattern in shades of brown and black, in a material so fine it could almost have been human hair. It clearly wasn't from any five-and-dime. It clearly wasn't made in Japan. It had been woven here, long, long ago, by women who lived in adobe pueblos and stood on

Spirit Rock watching their men ride off to battle.

I felt my heart hammering inside my chest. Dr. Delgado opened the basket cautiously. Inside it were what looked like tiny pebbles. He nodded to his assistants. "This is the grave of a person of importance," he said. "I would surmise a great medicine man." He got to his feet. "If the pattern is true to other burial sites of the ancient Pima, then I think we'll find several such graves up here."

"Does that mean that Spirit Rock really is an important Indian site?" Scott asked.

"Undoubtedly," Dr. Delgado said.

"And they won't be able to build their resort on it?" Scott insisted.

"I think that public opinion would be against destroying such a historical treasure," Dr. Delgado said. "I am going to take steps immediately to see that this hill is declared a historic monument of the Pima tribe."

"We've done it, Ginger!" Scott yelled excitedly. "You've done it! You were the one who found it! You're a genius! I love you!" He picked me up and swung me around in his strong arms. Sky and rock flashed past me, and all I could see was Scott's face, his blue eyes smiling down into mine. Had he really said "I love you"? Could this be happening to me?

Chapter 9

The rest of the morning passed in a daze. I might have been up on Spirit Rock for one hour or one day or one lifetime. All I could see was Scott's eyes laughing down into mine. I could feel his warm breath on my cheek and hear those words over and over: "I love you."

If this was one of my daydreams, I never wanted it to stop. I knew that this had gone beyond wanting to make Ben jealous. I didn't care if Ben ever came back from his football tournament. I was hopelessly, deeply, completely, and utterly in love with Scott Masters!

The only time I came out of my daydream for a second was when I heard a great roar of laughter from the excavation site. "Look what we've just found, Doctor!" one of the assistants shouted. "Someone buried a whole lot of junk right next to the grave site. Jennifer thought she'd made this major discovery and it turned out to say 'Made in Japan' on the back."

Everyone started laughing, and the assistant called Jennifer looked as if she wished the ground would open up and swallow her. I was really feeling bad for her when Scott nudged me and said, "Imagine thinking the ancient Pima drank their coffee out of Japanese cups." He grinned. "I wonder why anyone would bury a pile of junk way up here. It's a long way to go to get rid of garbage."

"Search me," I said. There was no way I was going to own up to knowing anything about the phony grave with Scott standing right beside me.

By midday things got pretty chaotic. Someone had gone down to send a message back to the museum and they must have alerted the media, because suddenly we were surrounded by cameras and microphones.

"I understand you're the young lady who made this important discovery," a dark-haired reporter asked. I recognized her from evening TV. She asked me a bunch of questions and then told me that they were planning to do a feature segment on "kids who make a difference," starring Scott and me. She asked if we could come down to the studio later in the day to tape interviews and put the piece together. I said I might have time to squeeze it into my busy schedule!

"You see, Ginger? Instant stardom," Scott teased. "I bet you never thought saving Spirit Rock would end up like this."

"Never in a million years," I agreed. Would my friends ever believe that I had saved Spirit Rock, become a celebrity, and made Scott Masters fall in love with me, all in the same day? I found it hard to believe myself.

I don't even remember coming down the mountain. I think I floated all the way. My feet didn't touch the rocky path once. Scott was there, so close that I brushed against him as we went through the narrow parts. I longed for him to take my hand, but I guess he felt that wouldn't be right. I mean, real archaeologists don't go around holding hands on the job, do they? But it was enough just to have him there beside me. When he spoke to me, his eyes positively glowed. My face was glowing, too. I must have looked like one huge grin as more and more people said nice things to me.

At the bottom, I stopped to pull up a couple of the stakes. "They won't be needing these anymore," I said. "I think I'll use them to start the barbecue."

Everyone applauded. I felt as if there was nothing in the world I couldn't do.

"Do you want a ride to the studio?" Scott asked.

"I'd like to go home and freshen up first," I said. "I want to look good for my one TV appearance in life."

"I think you look fine," he said.

"Maybe I should just comb my hair and put on some makeup," I suggested. "And change my shorts. These have dirt all over them."

"Okay," he said. "I'll drive you home and wait for you."

As we drove up, I saw that Ben's truck was already in the driveway. I couldn't believe my luck. *Now he'll see what happens when a guy ignores Ginger Hartman,* I told myself. This was my great moment of triumph, the moment that made up for the hurt I'd felt when I overheard that conversation in the locker room.

"I'll be right back," I called to Scott, jumping down from the Jeep. I flung open the front door and made my grand entrance. Todd and Ben weren't sitting on the living room sofa for once, which was kind of disappointing.

"Todd? Anybody home?" I yelled.

Instantly Todd appeared from his room. "Oh, you're back, finally," he said. "Ben's been driving me crazy, waiting for you to come home."

"I'm not stopping," I said. "I have to change quickly and get out of here—"

"You can't go out now," Todd said. "Ben has the most amazing news!"

"I have the most amazing news myself," I said.

"But wait until you hear Ben's news," Todd cut in. "Ben, get out here and tell her!"

Ben appeared from Todd's bedroom. "Hi, Ginger," he said. His face was glowing, just like Scott's. "Guess what? They put me in at wide receiver."

"And tell her the rest," Todd went on. He turned to me. "He scored the winning touchdown! He was amazing. He caught the pass, broke about five tackles, and went all the way—and we won the tournament!"

"Congratulations," I said, "but wait until you hear *my* news. I have just single-handedly saved Spirit Rock, and I'm going to be interviewed for a Channel 10 feature."

I waited for them to be impressed. Nothing happened. Disgusted, I started to push past them into my bedroom.

"When will you be back?" Ben asked.

"The guys are throwing a party in Ben's honor," Todd said. "You have to come."

I looked from my brother to Ben. "I have to come?" I repeated.

"Yeah . . . the guys will expect Ben to bring a

date," Todd went on, since Ben seemed reluctant to talk.

I could feel the anger boiling up inside me. "You expect me not to be interviewed by a TV station so that Ben can take me to a party? Is that what I'm hearing?"

"Of course not," Ben said hastily. "Go do your TV thing first. I'm sure it won't take more than a couple of minutes."

"Of course," I said, giving him my sweetest smile. "Why should anything I've done be worth more than a couple of minutes on TV? I mean, it's not like it's a winning touchdown or anything."

"Right," Todd agreed. He really is dumb sometimes.

"You guys make me sick," I snapped. "Last week you sneaked around behind my back so you could go to a party with a bunch of dumb cheerleaders and now suddenly you've decided that you want me around again, because Mr. Studly Wide Receiver needs a girl gazing at him adoringly to boost his image. Well, thanks, but no thanks. I'm not a book you can take off the shelf when it's convenient for you and put back when it's not. I'm a person, with feelings. And you know what?" I paused dramatically. "I don't even need you anymore, Ben Campbell. I have Scott waiting for me outside. That's *Scott,* as in Scott Masters—you know, the famous senior? He wouldn't sneak around behind my back to spend an evening with a bunch of cheerleaders."

I rushed into my room and shut the door in their astonished faces. Rapidly I threw everything I owned out of my drawers until I came up with a pair of shorts that didn't look wrinkled and my pale blue halter top. A little mascara, a healthy amount of blush . . . no time for a curling iron, but I caught up my ponytail with my best velvet scrunchie. A quick squirt of Giorgio that Roni had given me last Christmas, and I was ready.

I ran out again, past two dazed-looking guys. Apparently they didn't know what to do when a girl fought back and wanted her own way. Well, they should be used to this girl by now. I'd never taken any nonsense from either of them, and I wasn't about to start.

Ben got up and followed me to the front door. "Ginger, wait," he said. "I didn't mean to upset you. . . ."

I turned back to him. "Not last week? Not when I overheard you in the locker room saying that I meant nothing to you? That I was just a little kid? Well, Scott doesn't seem to think I'm a little kid. He thinks I'm pretty special."

I opened the front door. "Good-bye, Ben. Enjoy your party. Maybe you can find one of those dippy cheerleaders to go with you."

"He might just do that!" Todd yelled after me. But Ben didn't say anything as I ran out to the waiting Jeep.

The interview went great. Scott was an old pro in front of the cameras. He was cool and relaxed and I'm sure had every watching female under ninety-five drooling over him. Sitting beside him, I wasn't nervous either. It was incredible to have all these adults talking to me as if I was someone important. Dr. Delgado had been invited, but they hardly talked to him at all. They just let him hold the little basket and the beads for a close-up and then asked me to describe how I had found them. A lot of the interview focused on our ecology club at school and how kids can make a difference saving the environment.

"You were great," Scott said as we came out of the bright lights into the dingy hallway. "You weren't nervous at all."

"You were pretty good yourself."

"Yeah, well, I've done it a few times before," he said. "The first time is always scary. Now we have to get home in time to watch it on the six o'clock news."

This great picture came into my head: myself and Scott, snuggled together on the sofa at his house, munching chips and popcorn while we watched ourselves on TV and laughed and kidded around.

"I'm going to have to floor it if I want to get you home first and then make it back to my house," he said, completely bursting my bubble.

I opened my mouth to say that I could take the bus, but the words stuck in my throat. Was this the same guy who had told me he loved me a couple of hours ago?

I guess he must have seen my face, because he put an arm around my shoulders. "I have a good idea," he said. "Do you know Spanky's Pizza?"

"I think so," I said, not sure what was coming next. "Is that the place in the new Scottsdale mall?"

"Right. I go there a lot and a couple of my buddies work there. It has a giant-screen TV, so I was thinking—why don't we drive over there and watch ourselves on the big screen?"

"Oh, wow," I said. This was even better than my daydream. Me and Scott, together for all the world to see, watching ourselves on a giant TV while everyone around us looked on admiringly.

He took my hand. "Come on. Let's do it."

It was almost ten o'clock when I arrived home. My face was frozen into a big, contented smile. I had never, in my entire life, been the center of attention for so long. Of course, I did have to share the spotlight with Scott, but I didn't mind that. Would you mind sharing the spotlight with the world's most gorgeous guy?

It seemed like everyone in the pizza parlor knew him. Everyone clustered around us, making jokes as our faces loomed, way larger than life, across the wall. Everyone congratulated us and slapped us on the back for stopping the developers from taking over Spirit Rock.

"They should rename it after you, Scott," one of his buddies said.

Scott turned to me. "They should name it after Ginger," he said. "Ginger Rock."

"Sounds like a new kind of candy," someone said, and instantly there was loud laughter all around me. I had to pinch myself yet again to prove that I wasn't dreaming.

There were no lights on in the house when I climbed down from Scott's Jeep. "I had a wonderful time," I said. "Thanks a million for everything."

"No, thank you," he said. "You did it, Ginger. You saved Spirit Rock. And now that I know what you can do, I'm not going to let you escape from the ecology club again. There are big developers just waiting to gobble up every inch of open space around the city. I'm counting on you."

He reached out and touched my cheek. For a second I imagined that he was going to pull me toward him and kiss me, but he didn't. His hand brushed my cheek, then went back to the steering wheel.

"Do . . . uh . . . you want to come in for a while?" I tried to sound light and breezy as I said it, but I think I sounded more like Mickey Mouse. "We've got some good ice cream."

"Oh, no thanks. I should be getting back. My folks will be wondering where I've disappeared to," he said with an easy laugh. "See you at school. Good night, Ginger."

"Good night," I managed to say with a bright smile.

I walked up the driveway and into the dark house. If only I knew more about boys. Had he wanted to kiss me but been shy? Scott didn't strike me as the shy type. What did it mean when you touched a girl's cheek? That you liked her, surely. And he'd said that he loved me. People didn't say stuff like that without meaning it, right?

10

There were several messages on the answering machine—all for me. Some of them were from friends and neighbors to say they'd seen me on TV. Three were from Roni.

"Ginger!" the first one said. "I'm leaving for Karen's house in about an hour. Give me a call when you get back and my dad can drive us both over."

"Ginger!" the next one said. "I'm at Karen's. Where are you? It's dark now, so you can't still be up that dumb mountain. Don't tell me you went out with Scott? Hubba-hubba. Call us immediately, understand?"

"Ginger! We just saw you on TV! Ohmigosh, we were so excited! Karen's mom thought we'd freaked out the way we were dancing around. And then we heard how you discovered the grave. Ginger, we're all really uncomfortable. I don't think you should go through with this. I mean, I know we thought it was a good idea to begin with, and we all tried to convince you, but now we don't think it's so hot after all. Ginger—you can't let them go on believing that it's a real Native American grave. They're going to find out as soon as they test this stuff and they'll know you're a phony. Call me as soon as you hear this. And call the museum guys, too. You'll feel better when you've told the truth!"

I sat down on the sofa and started laughing as I dialed Karen's number. "Listen, you creeps," I said as soon as Karen picked up the phone. "You didn't really think your fake bones would fool anyone for a second, did you? I didn't. I went up there early to get rid of them and I found this real grave right next to where you had been digging."

I waited for the squeals to die down at the other end.

"So those things they showed on TV weren't Roni's beads?"

"Of course not. They're fourteenth-century clay beads."

Roni snatched the phone from Karen. "I told the others they looked old! I said I never let my stuff get dirty like that. So you really did it, Ginger? You really saved Spirit Rock forever?"

"It looks like it," I said. "Dr. Delgado from the museum is having their lawyers put a temporary stop on any further work until it's officially named a historical site. But he's sure it will be. No golf courses or shopping malls on Spirit Rock!"

"I bet your brother will be mad," Roni said, laughing. "No big tips for him and Ben."

"I couldn't care less what happens to him or to that jerk Ben," I said. I told her what had happened earlier this evening.

"Holy cow," Roni said. "We always thought Ben was one of the more sensitive guys around. He's as macho as the rest of them." Roni put on her football player voice. "What's a little old TV interview compared to having you stand behind me, gazing on adoringly while guys slap my back at a party!"

"I don't care," I said. "Ben is history. Why would I want him around when I've got the cutest guy in Arizona?"

There was a pause, then a gasp at the other end of the line. "It really worked? Scott did notice you today?"

"He's just dropped me off in his Jeep," I said smugly. "He stroked my cheek and said he wasn't going to let me walk out of his life again."

"You're putting me on, right?"

"I swear that's what happened."

I heard her telling the others, and then there were loud screams in the background. "Karen and Justine are happy for you," Roni said. "I'm happy, too. Imagine, Ginger—we wanted people to notice us. We dreamed of meeting boys. And now you've got *the* number-one guy in the entire school. Who would have thought you'd be the one to take Alta Mesa by storm?"

"It's pretty amazing," I said. "I'm still totally in shock, Roni."

"You deserve it," she said. "You worked hard to save Spirit Rock. You should be feeling so proud."

"Thanks," I said.

"I suppose you have no way of getting over here?" she asked. "It doesn't seem like a real sleepover without you."

"Nobody's home except me," I said. "And I'm kind of tired. Being a celebrity is pretty exhausting, you know."

"I bet," she said. "Okay, talk to you tomorrow, then. Will you have time to do stuff with us or will you be up on your rock again?"

"Back on Spirit Rock, I think. Dr. Delgado expects to find more grave sites."

"Oh. See you Monday, then," Roni said in a very quiet voice (for her). "We thought we might all rent Rollerblades and try them in the park tomorrow."

"Oops! I forgot about your Rollerblading adventure. How was it?"

"It was great! I was actually pretty good. Drew fell down a couple of times, but I didn't, not once. He got mad at me, because I could turn and skate backward. He said obviously I could only do it well because little girls spend their time roller-skating, while guys are playing football and baseball."

I laughed. "I guess all guys have fragile egos where girls are concerned," I said. I thought of Ben as I said it and an uncomfortable feeling ran through me.

After I hung up the phone, I flung myself down on my bed. I wasn't going to let anything tip me from the high I was feeling. *The most perfect day of my life,* I thought. I'd not only saved Spirit Rock and gotten Scott to notice me. I'd been the first one to make my mark at a new high school—me, Ginger, the one with straight hair and freckles and no designer clothes. I grinned to myself in the darkness. And this was only the beginning. From now on things would get better and better!

I was right. The dream continued all week. On Sunday we found some Indian petroglyphs (that's rock paintings) in an overhang on the rock. That brought the media up again, and again they mentioned how I was the one who started the whole thing.

When I got to school on Monday morning, it seemed as if all three thousand students had been watching the TV news. I couldn't walk two yards down the hall without someone saying, "Hey, weren't you the one I saw on TV?"

Teachers I didn't even know stopped me in the halls and said nice things to me. A social studies teacher said she was looking forward to having me in her class next year. A civics teacher said he'd have to take some pointers from me on how to fight city hall. I suppose with all this attention, it was only natural that it went to my head a little. That's the only way I can explain what happened later in the week.

On Sunday, Dr. Delgado had said that the one problem he saw with preserving Spirit Rock was lack of funds. His museum had no funds available for putting in trails and preserving the petroglyphs from vandals. Rangers would be needed, and interpretive signs and benches for people to sit on, and a real parking lot . . . and all of this would cost megabucks. That was when Scott volunteered our ecology club. He said we'd start a campaign to get corporate sponsors for the rock. We'd write to all the big companies in town and get them to buy a bench, or pay for a trail that would be named after them.

I thought this sounded like a great idea—until I

saw how much work it would be. On Monday the ecology club met and Scott tried to hand out assignments. "I thought we'd divide the list of companies between us and each write to one page on the list," he said.

This produced an instant reaction. "I'd love to help, you know that, Scott, but I've got a big exam coming up and I have to get a good grade."

"This week just isn't great for me. I've got volleyball practice after school . . ."

"I have a paper due for English . . ."

They were all good excuses.

"It's okay," Scott said. "I know I can count on Ginger to help out."

He gave me his wonderful smile and I found myself nodding.

"After all, it's her project," someone muttered from the back of the room. I got the feeling that they might be jealous of all my publicity.

So I started addressing envelopes, sticking on stamps until my tongue felt like sandpaper. But it was worth it to be working beside Scott. He only had to say, "You're the greatest, Ginger," and I melted like an ice cream cone. I would willingly have licked stamps for the next U.S. census if he'd asked me to.

I did notice that he was coming to rely on me more and more. "Ginger, where did we leave that directory?

Would you be an angel and get it for me?" . . . "Ginger, if you happen to be going near a mailbox, could you just drop these off?" I decided this was great. Soon Scott wouldn't be able to get along without me.

I tried not to think about Ben at all, because when I did, I couldn't stop myself from feeling guilty—as if I'd let him down in some way, rather than the opposite. *He let me down first,* I kept telling myself. *He put me down and went to the party with the cheerleaders. He didn't care about my feelings.*

But none of this really made me feel better. Especially not after Wednesday afternoon. I bumped into him as he was dropping off Todd from football practice and he said, "I saw you on TV, Ginger. I thought you looked really good. You answered the questions well, too."

"Thanks," I muttered, and turned to go into the house.

"Now that you're a big celebrity, I guess you won't have any time for your old friends," he called after me. I knew that he was talking about himself. I heard the worry in his voice, but I pretended I didn't.

"I'm kind of busy on the sponsorship campaign," I replied breezily. "You know, we're getting corporate sponsors, contacting all the big companies in the city."

But I found that I couldn't look at him.

"Well, gotta run," I said. "I promised Scott I'd address a lot of envelopes tonight."

I didn't look back as Ben revved the truck and drove away fast. *He started it,* I told myself again and again. And anyone would be a fool to turn down the most successful guy in the school, wouldn't they? Ben would have to understand that relationships came to an end. I'd moved on to bigger and better things.

I had thought my friends would be happy for me, but they weren't too crazy about the amount of time I was spending with Scott. In fact, apart from my bus ride in with Roni, I hardly had time to see my friends all week. Each day I ran from class to meet Scott and get started on my tasks for the day. I thought my friends would understand. I thought they'd be happy that I'd finally ended up with the guy of my dreams. I would have been happy if it had happened to one of them. But each time I bumped into them, they didn't look happy at all.

"Sorry, guys, gotta run," I said as Karen started talking to me while I crammed stuff into my locker at lunchtime on Friday.

"Don't tell me you've got to help Scott again," she said, glancing across at Roni. "We never get to see you these days."

"You know how it is when you're famous!" I said with my light, celebrity laugh. "It's all go, go, go. I'm sorry you'll have to do without my company, but this mailing to corporate sponsors is really important. We hope to get the last batch of letters out today. Did I mention that Scott said we might have to meet with some of these corporate sponsors? And did I mention that one of the sponsors might just be the Suns? How about a poster with Ginger and Sir Charles on it? Or Ginger and Dan Maherle? It could say: 'We're in this together for Spirit Rock!' Yeah, I like that. You want my autograph now, before you have to wait in line for it?"

My friends were looking at me as if they weren't sure whether or not I was joking.

Karen laughed nervously. "Oh, I think we'll wait and take our chances," she said, with a quick look at Roni. "You're such a kidder, Ginger."

Was I kidding? I wasn't even sure myself. I wondered if I was turning into another Justine. I just opened my mouth and these incredible things came out. I really didn't mean to brag, but as I heard myself, I knew that's exactly what I was doing.

"Just give me a week to enjoy my glory," I said with a lame grin.

"I wouldn't call it glory, sticking stamps on envelopes," Roni said.

"You're just jealous because you're not sitting with Scott every lunch hour," I said smugly. "And because you didn't get to be on TV and have everyone in school know your name."

She didn't answer, but that night as we rode the bus home, Roni said, "I don't suppose you'll be sleeping over at my house tomorrow."

"Why not?" I was surprised.

She looked at me coldly. "A big celebrity like you? I assumed you'd have more important things to do, like polish Scott's Jeep."

"What's that supposed to mean?"

"Ginger, you've spent the entire week doing things for Scott," Roni said. "Every time I've passed you in the halls, you're running to find him a book, or to mail letters for him."

"You make it sound like I'm his slave," I said, my cheeks turning pink.

"Well, aren't you?"

"Scott and I are partners. We're working together to get the rock financed by corporations. That takes a lot of effort, you know."

"I'm sure it does," Roni said, her face still expressionless. "Only, it seems that Scott is the one with all the great ideas and you're the one who puts in all the effort."

"That's not true at all!" I snapped. "We've both been working our guts out—"

"Then how did I happen to see Scott in the cafeteria

with a bunch of seniors while you were in a room addressing envelopes all lunch hour?"

"So? He went to grab a bite to eat," I said. "What's wrong with that? I had my lunch with me, so I didn't need to leave."

"How convenient," Roni said. "I hope he brought you back one of those cookies he was eating. He was feeding them to all the girls at his table."

My face had turned from pink to red. "You know what?" I demanded. "You really are jealous. You can't handle the fact that I'm finally the one in the spotlight. You can't handle the fact that I'm a celebrity around school and I've snagged myself a total babe. You didn't believe that a nobody like me could get a guy like Scott."

"I'd be happy if you got him," Roni said, "but I think he's just using you. All this publicity has gone to your head, Ginger. I want you to see sense before you make a big fool of yourself."

"A fool of myself? It's you who's making a fool of yourself right now," I stormed. "Scott says that he and I are on the same wavelength. He says it's amazing the way I know what he's thinking. . . ."

"I think you've got a giant crush on him and he's using that to get you to act as his gofer," Roni said.

"You don't know anything about it," I said icily. "For your information, Scott has already suggested that we do something together this weekend. So maybe you're right. Maybe I'll be too busy to come to your childish sleepover."

"Oh, so now you find our sleepovers childish?" Roni was yelling now, making people in the seats ahead of us turn around and stare.

I was so riled up, I didn't notice that I was yelling back. "Let's face it, Roni! They are totally immature! Silly games and childish boyfriend clubs and throwing popcorn around—"

"Fine, so don't come."

"Fine. I won't," I said.

There was a silence. Then she said, "Ginger, what's gotten into you? It's not like you to talk like this."

I looked away from her. "Maybe I've outgrown you guys," I said. "Now that I'm hanging out with more mature people like Scott, I've grown up, and you're still little kids."

"Fine, if that's the way you want it," Roni said. She sat staring straight ahead of her until we reached our stop. Then she walked in her direction and I walked in mine. That wasn't the way I wanted it at all, but I didn't know what to say to make things right.

11

I didn't sleep well that night. It wasn't as if Roni and I had never fought before. When we were little, we were always having the sort of fights where we yelled: "Am not." "Are too." "Am not." "Are too," until one of us went home in tears. But since we'd grown up, we'd gotten along pretty well. We'd had our differences, but never a cold, silent parting of the ways like today.

I had never thought that Roni would turn out to be the jealous type. I'd imagined she would be happy for me, the way I would have been happy for her. I hadn't done anything wrong, for pete's sake! It's not like I tried to be famous and get on TV. I had just wanted to save Spirit Rock! And after all, she had Drew, who was definitely one of the cutest guys in the school. So why should she get so uptight about me and Scott? Maybe she was jealous that I was dating a senior. Maybe she was scared that I really would start moving with an older crowd now and leave her out in the cold.

"Let her see if she can survive without me," I told myself, frowning into the darkness. "Just wait until she wants some help with her math homework. Just wait until she's in her house alone and she hears a scary noise and she wants me to come over. She'll come running back, begging me to forgive her."

I thought this would make me feel better, but it didn't. My stomach felt as if it had a big, gaping hole in it. I got up and put on my favorite Mariah Carey CD, but it didn't relax me the way it usually did. It was past midnight when I finally fell asleep.

I woke up later than I expected. Everyone was probably up on Spirit Rock, wondering where I was. I grabbed the nearest shorts and T-shirt and ran into the kitchen to find a bagel. On the fridge was a note from my father: GONE FISHING WITH HARRY BRONTSON. MAY BE BACK VERY LATE TONIGHT. LEAVE CHAIN OFF DOOR.

His truck was still in the driveway as I hurried past. They'd obviously gone in Harry's old camper. This was my dad's ideal way of spending a weekend—up by a lake, line dangling in the water, grilled fish over a campfire, communing with nature. Maybe that's where I got my Spirit Rock genes from.

There was a lot of activity as I climbed up Spirit Rock. Johnny came past me with a tray of sodas.

"Hey, waiter, why is the service so slow around here?" I teased as he hurried past.

"This is about all they'll let me do," he complained. "They've got the professionals in today, and they're not letting us near the sites."

I was sure that wouldn't apply to me, Ginger Hartman, preserver of Spirit Rock and discoverer of the first grave. I continued up the track and picked my way over to where two older women were working.

"How's it going?" I asked, squatting beside them.

"Don't get too close, honey," one of them said, scarcely looking up. "There's a lot of fragile stuff around here."

"I know," I said. "I found the first grave." But I don't think they even heard me. I went on up the trail, looking for Scott. He wasn't anywhere around. Two men told me to be careful where I was walking.

"Who allowed all these kids up here?" I heard one of them growl.

"Who allowed you on my rock?" I said, not loudly enough for anyone to hear.

As I went back down I saw some familiar faces—Elaine and another girl from the ecology club. They were sitting together at a trestle table making sandwiches.

"So are you going to Scott's party tonight?" the other girl asked Elaine.

"Of course. Are you?"

"I haven't decided yet. Do you think it will be fun or one of his serious save-the-planet parties?"

"Fun," Elaine said. "His folks are out of town."

I could feel my face getting very hot. As casually as I could I walked up to them. "So . . . uh . . . where is Scott today? I don't see him around."

"I think he said he was meeting with one of the sponsors," Elaine said, giving me a sweet smile.

"Oh," was all I could say. Scott had let me think that when we met sponsors, it would be the two of us.

"I'm sure he'll show up later," Elaine said with another condescending smile. "If you've got nothing to do, you can help slice tomatoes for these sandwiches."

"Thanks, but I think I'll go find Dr. Delgado and see how he's getting along," I said.

I heard them say something to each other in low voices as I turned away, and then there was a little chuckle. *They were jealous, too,* I told myself. They'd been jealous of me since I came into the room and stole their limelight. Well, I might just find another spectacular grave today, to remind them all that Ginger Hartman was still here.

I clambered over rocks and scrub, looking for a likely place, but all I got was scratched legs. When I finally twisted my ankle on a loose rock, I came down to earth in more ways than one. I sat there among the rocks and prickles, waiting for somebody to come help me, but nobody came. Gradually it dawned on me that I wasn't important. I wasn't being missed. Nobody cared if I fell and hurt myself. As I tried to get up, I thought of Ben and his story about being a Cub Scout on the rock. Poor Ben. I had laughed when I'd heard it, but it must have been scary to a little kid to lie among the rocks, waiting for somebody to come help him up again.

Cautiously I put weight on my ankle and got to my feet. There was no real damage . . . except to my ego. *Face it, Ginger,* I told myself, *you wouldn't recognize a grave site from a picnic site.* Okay, so I wasn't Ginger the great explorer. I was Ginger, the ordinary person. Everything that happened to me last week had been pure luck . . . except that Scott really had been interested in me, hadn't he? In my mind I went over and over the way he smiled at me, the nice things he said, and the way his hand had touched my cheek. So if he liked me, how come he was having a party and he hadn't invited me?

I hung around on the rock most of the day, waiting for Scott to show up. By afternoon, when everyone was packing up, I finally decided he wasn't coming and headed back home. It was still early enough to go over to Roni's and join my friends for a sleepover. Part of me really wanted to, but then I remembered how Roni had stormed off last night. I wasn't going to go crawling back to ask her forgiveness when I hadn't done anything wrong.

Besides, there was somewhere else I wanted to be. It took half an hour of staring at the phone before I finally got up the nerve to dial Scott's number. I'd rehearsed my speech hundreds of times. I knew exactly what I was going to say to him. Even so, when I heard his voice on the other end of the line, my heart started pounding so hard that I could scarcely breathe.

"Hi, Scott, it's Ginger," I managed to gasp.

"Hey, Ginger. What's up?" He sounded relaxed and confident as ever.

"I was wondering why you weren't at Spirit Rock today. I hope nothing was wrong."

"I didn't see any point in coming," he said. "It's all up to the pros now. I felt I'd just be in the way. So I went over to Allied Chemicals to see if they'd like to be a sponsor, and they might be interested."

"That's great," I said.

There was a pause while I wondered where the conversation was going from here. "So, um, Scott, what are you doing tonight?"

What a jerk I was! Why did I say that? I didn't mean to blurt it out like that at all. I meant to be cool and subtle.

"Me? Nothing much. Just having a few friends over."

"Oh. Okay."

Another pause.

"Hey, you know you're welcome to come if you want."

"I am?"

"Sure. I meant to tell you about it at school yesterday, but we've been so busy this week, it slipped my mind."

"That's okay, I understand."

"So come on over if you want. It's nothing special. We're just going to hang out, get some pizza . . . I guess people will start arriving around eight. You know where I live?"

"I have your address."

"You can't miss it. There's an adobe wall around the yard with black iron lamps on it. Well, I better go clean up this place before anyone gets here. See you later, maybe?"

"Sure. I'll be there."

I was smiling to myself as I put down the phone. He had meant to tell me about it, but we'd been so busy. There was only one small problem—I had to find a way to get across town on a Saturday night. Most buses didn't run this late. My dad was up at some lake fishing. I just had to hope that my brother showed up soon and was in a good enough mood to drive me over to Scott's. Maybe he would if I promised to do his laundry for a month.

I fixed myself a grilled cheese sandwich. I showered and put on my best white jeans and my one silky blouse. I brushed my hair and made up my face. I looked pretty darned sexy, I decided, and not at all like a freshman. Maybe this would do the trick with Scott. Maybe he'd look up as I came into the room and his eyes would sparkle and he'd say, "Ginger, I'm so glad you came . . ." and nobody else would stand a chance with him all evening.

Seven o'clock came and there was no Todd. I hadn't a clue where he was. The only person who would know was Ben, and I wasn't going to call his house to find out. I could hardly ask him to drive me, either. So I waited. And waited. It was almost eight o'clock. Obviously Todd and Ben were out for the night, probably at another football party with all the dumb cheerleaders.

I paced up and down. If I called Scott and said I needed a ride, would he come and get me? What if he said that he couldn't leave his party guests . . . what if that made him mad and he didn't like me anymore? I knew I'd be rushing around like crazy if kids were about to show up for a party at my house. I didn't have the nerve to call him again, anyway.

I went through my address book three times. Wasn't there anyone—family friend, distant relative—who would be happy to drive me across town? Nobody. Then I got the phone book and started looking in the yellow pages for taxis. After the first call I knew it would cost at least fifteen dollars. Okay, and then a possible fifteen dollars back. Thirty dollars! The only place I had thirty dollars was in my savings account.

So I was stuck out here in the boonies, too far to ride my bike and without a ride to the party of my life. It didn't seem fair. After all that good luck last week, now I was whammied with bad luck just when I was about to snag the cutest guy at Alta Mesa.

You've got to go for it, Ginger, I told myself. *If you want it to happen badly enough, it will happen. . . .* That's when it came to me: there was a perfectly good truck standing in the driveway and I knew where the spare keys were. *You're crazy,* I told myself. *You don't even have a license.*

But I know how to drive, a little voice answered me. Todd had let me drive his car on several occasions, around the big muddy field beside our house, around our church parking lot. It was easy. It wasn't as if the truck was any different—it was just a big, high-up car. I could handle it if I stayed off the freeway and kept to empty side streets. I could just imagine Scott's face when I arrived.

"How did you get here?"

"Oh, I drove. That's my truck outside."

Perfect. Totally perfect. I just had to do it. Before I could stop myself, I'd found the spare keys in the drawer and I was sitting on the cold vinyl of the truck seat. I turned the key and the engine roared to life. At that point I began to get a little scared. The truck seemed much bigger than I remembered—impossibly high off the ground.

"You can do this," I told myself. "You have good coordination and you know the way . . . it's a piece of cake."

But it didn't feel like a piece of cake as I took off the parking brake and the truck surged forward like a powerful wild animal. "Whoa!" I yelled, braking so hard that I was flung into the steering wheel. This time I took the brake off slowly and inched forward, the gravel of the driveway crunching beneath the monster tires.

I swung the wheel around and turned out of the driveway and into the street, one wheel bumping over the far curb. Going straight was easy. I saw the lights on in Roni's bedroom as I passed her house. I resisted the desire to honk. I could imagine their surprised faces as they came to the window and saw me, Ginger the Indian princess, controlling this powerful monster by myself.

When I turned from our street onto the highway leading toward the city, I didn't even go over the curb. I'd gotten the hang of this driving business pretty well. Now as long as I stayed cool and drove slowly, I'd be fine. No problems.

A car passed me, driving fast. For a second the headlights blinded me. The road disappeared and I couldn't tell if I was going straight or not. The driver slowed, then sped on again. My hands were shaking on the wheel. I hadn't thought about cars coming from the opposite direction.

A pair of headlights came up from behind me, blinding me as they bounced off the rearview mirror. I slowed to a crawl. There was the blare of a horn and then an impatient driver screeched past me, almost forcing me into the ditch.

"Road hog!" I yelled, but he was long gone.

Luckily there were no other cars in sight. Black trees slipped past me as the glow of the city came nearer and nearer. It would be easier driving where there were streetlights. No more scares with blinding headlights, no more narrow country road with only just enough room to pass.

Then suddenly there was something in the road ahead. My headlights caught the gleam of eyes. A petrified dog crouched there, frozen.

It all happened in a second. I swerved to miss the dog, I felt the wheel jerk in my hands, and there was a bump and a jerk as the truck bucked like a bronco. My head banged against the windshield. *Seat belt!* I thought, a second too late. The front wheels of the truck slid into the ditch.

12

For a while I lay there, slumped against the steering wheel, too terrified to move. The engine was still rumbling and I turned it off, scared of possible gas tank rupture and fire. The following silence was even scarier. One headlight had gone out, and the other was shining at a crazy angle into the tree branches. I didn't know if I was up or down or what to do next. I examined the hand I'd used to switch off the engine. At least it still worked and had five fingers. That was a good sign.

Very cautiously I moved the various parts of my body, one by one. A few parts of me throbbed, but at least they all worked. I could walk back to Oak Creek and get help. I tried opening my door, but either it was jammed or I wasn't strong enough to open it. I turned sideways and tried kicking it, but my foot hurt.

"Someone will come," I said out loud. "Lots of cars come along this road."

Then I began to think about what would happen when somebody did come. They'd call the police and the police would ask to see my license. Did they put you in jail for driving without a license? It didn't really matter, because my dad was going to ground me for twenty years anyway. He'd probably never let me apply for my permit. All my friends would learn to drive and I'd be eighteen and still a passenger. . . .

A big tear squeezed itself out of my eye and down my cheek. "It wasn't my fault," I whispered. "I didn't want to kill that little animal. I was just being considerate, and now I'm going to be punished for it." But at the back of my mind another voice was whispering. *You acted like a dumb kid,* it said. *You stole your father's truck and now you've wrecked it, all so you could get to a party and impress Scott.*

Okay, so I'd been the world's biggest idiot. I didn't want to be grown up anymore. I wanted to be a little kid again and have my daddy come rescue me. I didn't even care that I'd be punished. I just wanted his arms around me.

"Daddy? Where are you?" I said into the darkness. "Somebody please come."

That's when I saw the headlights coming up behind me. They were big and bright, and they slowed until they pulled off the road behind the truck. It had to be the police. I was both scared and relieved.

"I'm sorry, Officer," I said as big hands wrenched open my door. "It was an accident. A dog ran out in front of me and before I knew where I was—"

"Ginger? Are you okay? What the heck were you doing?" I wasn't looking at a police officer at all. I was looking straight at Ben.

Tears of relief sprang to my eyes. "Oh, Ben, I'm so glad to see you," I said. "How did you know where to look for me?"

"We passed you on the road as we were driving home," Ben said. "Todd thought he saw his dad's truck. When we got home and found you gone, we had a hunch it was you in the truck, so Todd looked for the spare keys." He reached up to me. "Are you okay? Here, give me your hand." His arms came around me as he lifted me tenderly down to the ground.

"Is she okay?" a voice asked from the darkness. I saw Roni, Karen, and Justine standing there with my brother. Roni ran up to me.

"Ginger, are you hurt? Do you want us to call the paramedics?"

"I think I'm all right," I said. "Just shook up. I was so scared—"

"What on earth made you take your dad's truck?" Roni demanded, sounding mad now, the way parents do when they're relieved that you're okay. "You don't know how to drive."

"Do too," I said. "Ask Todd. I've driven his car enough."

"Around a parking lot, maybe," Todd said, storming over to inspect the damage, "but that's a long way from driving a strange truck at night. Where were you going that was so important?"

I felt my face burning. "To a party," I said. "I'd been invited to a party and I had no way of getting there."

"Scott Masters's party?" Ben demanded.

I nodded.

"What a creep," he said. "Any guy who invites a girl to a party and then doesn't have the decency to come pick her up is a lowlife in my book."

"That's not fair," I said. I swallowed hard. "He didn't really invite me like that . . . not me particularly . . . in fact, I sort of invited myself. So don't blame Scott. I was the dumb one."

"You sure were," Ben said. He glanced across at Todd, who was still scrambling around the truck. "How bad is it?"

"I think it's still drivable if we can get it out of the ditch. There's a headlight out and a dent on the fender. I'm sure there will be a lot of scratches on the paintwork, but otherwise she was pretty lucky."

"I'll say," Ben said, staring into the dark. "A few more inches and you'd have crashed into that tree, Ginger. The paramedics would have been pulling your body out just about now."

"Don't," I said, shivering. "Can we go home? I'm not feeling too great."

"Drive her back to my house," Roni said. "We'll take care of her."

"She's probably in shock," Karen said.

"She'll probably need therapy to help her through the trauma," Justine added. "My dad knows a great shrink—"

"Justine, shut up," Roni said. "What she needs is hot chocolate and bed." She put her arm around my shoulders. "Come on, let's get you home."

"I'll stay with the truck, in case the police show up," Ben said. He looked at Todd. "If you come right back with a tow rope, maybe we can get this baby out and working again."

"You think you could get it back in the driveway before Dad gets home?" I asked. "Maybe he won't even notice. . . ."

"He'll notice," Todd said dryly.

"There goes my chance to drive for the next four years." I sighed.

"I would say there goes your chance to leave the house again for the next four years," Todd said. "He loved that truck, Ginger. It was his pride and joy. You're going to be in a heap of trouble when he finds out."

"Don't make her feel any worse than she already does, Todd," Ben said. "It happened and there's nothing we can do to change that now. Why don't you get her home before she keels over and see if we can get the truck out of the ditch before the police show up?"

Like a sleepwalker, I stumbled beside Roni and Karen into Todd's car. A few minutes later I was in Roni's cozy bedroom with the lamp throwing a pink glow on a floor full of sleeping bags.

"Tea or hot chocolate?" Roni asked. "Or do you want me to run a bath for you first?"

She looked so worried that the tears I'd been holding back finally made their way to the surface. Karen put an arm around me. "It's okay now, you're safe," she said.

"We'll take care of you," Justine added.

"You're all being so nice to me," I said, "after I was such a jerk, especially to you, Roni. I'm so sorry about all those horrible things I said."

"It's okay," she muttered. "You just weren't yourself this week. This Spirit Rock thing went to your head."

"We understand," Karen said. "It's pretty heady stuff being on TV and having Scott Masters pay attention to you, all in one week."

"You've led such a boring life until now," Justine chirped brightly. "Obviously you weren't prepared to handle the spotlight the way I would have been."

"Justine, shut up," Roni and Karen said in unison. I looked at them and grinned. A few moments ago I had felt that I'd never smile again. It felt so good to be with my friends and to realize that they cared about me.

"You're right," I said. "I did let it go to my head. I loved all that attention. I loved being a somebody."

"Who wouldn't?" Karen said kindly.

I looked down at my hands. "I think I was only fooling myself about Scott Masters," I said in a small voice. "Ben was right. If he really cared about me, he would have come to pick me up, or at least made sure I had a ride. He was just using me as a willing slave, like you said, Roni."

"You had a monster crush on him, that's all," Roni said. "It's understandable. He *is* the cutest guy in the school, and he's a senior. I might have lost my marbles if he'd paid attention to me."

"Not you," I said. "You're too sensible, and you've got Drew. Who'd want Scott Masters when they've got Drew? Scott might be cute, but he doesn't have Drew's sense of humor. He takes things way too seriously."

Karen looked out the window. "I see lights," she said. "I wonder if that's the boys with the truck."

"How did you guys know that I'd taken the truck?" I asked.

"Todd and Ben showed up here, wondering if we knew where you were," Roni said. "We knew you'd been home until a little while ago because we'd seen the light in your bedroom window when we went out to look for the dog."

"The dog? Midnight is missing?"

"Don't worry. He'll come back. He always does," Roni said.

I felt a cold shiver down my back. "I bet it was your dog I almost hit," I said. "That's why I ran off the road. I swerved to miss an animal."

"Well, that's one good thing that's come out of this evening," Roni said. "You might have wrecked the truck, but you saved Midnight's life."

"I'm glad there's one good thing," I said. "Roni, I'm going to be in such big trouble. How can I ever pay for the truck to be fixed? And what about insurance? They might cancel my dad's insurance if they find out an unlicensed driver has been using his truck . . . and they'll never give me insurance now. . . ."

"Don't worry," Roni said. "It will sort itself out in the morning. There's nothing you can do about it now."

She installed me on her bed and tucked a blanket around me, then went to make me hot chocolate. When I tried to hold it, I found that my hands were still shaking.

"Here," Roni said, and she fed it to me like a baby. I sipped obediently, feeling the hot liquid gradually warming me. Suddenly I was aware of being watched. I looked up and there was Ben, standing in the doorway.

"How are you feeling?" he asked.

"Better now," I said. "What about the truck?"

"It's back in your driveway," Ben said. "We parked it with the dented side to the fence, so that your dad won't freak out until tomorrow."

"Thanks." I looked up at him. "Thank you for everything, Ben."

Ben cleared his throat. "It's okay. I'm just glad you're all right, Ginger."

"I just remembered," Roni said loudly. "That show we wanted to watch on TV is just starting." She pushed past Ben, handing him the hot chocolate on her way out.

"Oh, great," Karen said, leaping up. "I wouldn't miss it for the world."

"What show?" Justine asked. "You never said anything about a TV show. . . ."

"In the living room, Justine," Karen said, grabbing her and yanking her out of the room.

Ben stood by the door, holding the hot chocolate. He came over slowly and perched at the foot of the bed.

"Todd and I were doing some thinking," he said at last. "I think the best way out of this is to tell your dad that I was driving the truck."

"You? Why should you get in trouble for something I did?"

"Listen a minute," he said. "It makes sense, Ginger. I'm a licensed driver. I've got insurance. We'll tell your dad that I was driving you to a get-together for the Spirit Rock thing, because you had no other way of getting there, and an animal ran out in front of us, which is true. Accidents happen, you know. He might be mad at me for taking his truck, but you can say that you begged me until I gave in. I'll let you get in trouble for that much."

I was gazing up at him, at his soft, warm eyes behind those Clark Kent glasses. He had to be the sweetest person in the whole world. "I can't let you do this," I said.

"You have to. It's the only way," Ben said. "Your dad will be mad, but his insurance will pay and that will be that. At least this way you don't lose your chance for driving until you turn eighteen."

"I don't see why you're doing all this for me," I muttered.

"Ginger, you know I'd do anything for you," he said simply.

Our eyes met. "You still care about me?" I asked shakily.

"You know I care about you."

"No, I don't," I said. "I thought it was all over between us. I thought you were just finding a polite way to dump me."

"Me? Dump you? Why would you think that?"

"Because I heard you in the locker room," I reminded him. "I heard you tell the other guys that I didn't matter to you. I was just a little kid who was hanging around you."

He looked really embarrassed. "You shouldn't believe anything you hear in locker rooms," he said.

"So why did you say it?"

"Ginger, you know how it is," he said. "I'm a new guy on the team. I want them to like me. I didn't want them to think I was some kind of wimp who couldn't go to a party because his girlfriend wouldn't let him. I just said what they wanted to hear. I didn't think . . ." He looked up at me. "It was a boring party. I didn't enjoy it one bit. I left before midnight. I'm sorry."

Ben suddenly stood and began pacing the room. He took a deep breath. "You don't know how mad at myself I was. I thought I'd really blown it with you—

especially after Scott Masters. I mean heck, Ginger. How can a guy like me compete with Scott Masters?"

"There's no competition," I said. "You win hands down, Ben. Scott might care about saving piping plovers and Indian graves, but he uses people. I was his unpaid gofer, that's all."

"That's all?" Ben asked in a surprised voice. "But I thought . . . I mean, the way it sounded . . ."

"I wanted to make you jealous," I told him. "I thought you might not dump me if you thought Scott Masters was interested in me."

"Why would I want to dump you?"

"Because I'm just a freshman and you're the star wide receiver now."

"You didn't seem to think so last week," he said. "I didn't think what I did was important to you."

"I'm sorry. I didn't realize until now. You were so excited about your touchdown, and all I was interested in was my TV spot."

"I felt bad afterward, too," he said with a sheepish grin. "I was all wrapped up in my touchdown and I didn't think how excited you were about being on TV. I guess it takes time to learn how to put another person first. It's easy to fall in love with someone, but it takes work to keep on loving them."

I nodded. "It's just so hard for me to know what you're thinking and how I'm supposed to act."

"I feel the same way," he said. "Girls are still a mystery to me."

"And boys are a total mystery to me, even though I grew up surrounded by them."

"So are you ready to be Sherlock Holmes?" Ben asked. He slid his hand along the comforter until his fingers were wrapped around mine.

"Elementary, my dear Watson," I said.

He leaned toward me and gave me a gentle kiss.

"Oh, Ben," I whispered, tears filling my eyes. "I've missed you so much."

"This last week was the most miserable of my life," he whispered back.

Then his arms came around me and he held me tight. I felt safe, loved, and wonderful.

From outside the door came Justine's high voice. "I just want to get my—"

"Justine, don't go in there!" two voices warned.

"But I still don't see why we want to watch a rerun of 'The Partridge Family'!" she protested.

Ben and I gazed into each other's eyes and smiled.

Before he left, I had come to a decision. "Ben, there is no way I'm going to let you take the rap for what I did," I told him. "I'm the one who deserves to get into trouble. I have to face up to my dad or I'll never feel good about myself again. I know I'll probably be grounded until I'm ninety-nine, but will you come hold my hand through the bars of my window?"

Ben laughed and ruffled my hair. "I'll even bring you your favorite candy bars," he said. "But seriously, Ginger, the offer still stands. I don't mind taking the blame for you."

"But I mind." I sighed. "I've never lied to my dad before, and I'm not about to start now. If he found out, he'd never trust me again."

Ben nodded. "I understand. I'd feel the same way if I were you. Good luck, then. Call and tell me how it went."

"If I'm allowed telephone privileges," I said with an attempt at a smile. I was just beginning to realize how it might go. My dad wasn't always a mild-mannered, even-tempered guy. But I couldn't back down now.

The next morning I was waiting for my dad when he came out of his bedroom to get the morning paper.

"Hi, Dad," I said. "I've already made you coffee, and I can do waffles if you want."

He looked at me suspiciously. "What do you want, an advance on your allowance again?"

"No, Dad," I said. "It's more serious than that. I just want you to promise that whatever I tell you, you won't stop loving me. Because I love you, honestly, and I'm very, very sorry, and I'll take whatever punishment you give me."

The scowl faded from his face. "What is it, Ginger? Are you in some kind of trouble?"

I nodded. I couldn't even speak.

"What is it? You can tell your old dad," he said.

I shook my head and tears started to well up in my eyes. "Come outside and I'll show you," I managed to stammer. Looking puzzled, he followed me.

I walked around to the side of the truck and pointed, silently. In the bright sunlight it looked pretty bad—an ugly gash along the new paintwork and a crumpled mess where the headlight used to be.

"My truck!" he yelled. "What happened to my truck? Were you out driving with some crazy boy?"

"No, Dad. It was me."

He turned to look at me. "But you're only fourteen. You can't drive."

"I know that now," I said. "I don't know what came over me. I was just so desperate to get to Scott's house for a party. I thought it would be easy. It really wasn't far, and it was all back roads with not much traffic on them . . . but then a dog ran out in front of me and I swerved and lost control."

"My truck," he said again. "My beautiful new truck."

"I almost hit a tree," I interrupted. "I could have

been killed, Dad. It could have been worse."

He looked at me long and hard. Finally he nodded. "You're right. It could have been worse," he said. "And I think you've learned your lesson, haven't you?"

"You bet," I agreed. "No more driving until I get my permit and have you with me." I said this with a hopeful smile, just in case he was about to say, "No permit until you turn twenty-one."

"This is going to cost money," he said at last.

"I know that. I'll try to pay what I can." I gulped. "You can put it on a tab and I'll pay you back as soon as I'm old enough to get a real job."

His arm slid around my shoulders. "That's okay, honey. That's why I have insurance," he said. "Even good drivers have to swerve to avoid animals sometimes."

I gazed up at him. "Thanks, Dad. You don't know how scared I was to tell you this."

"But you told me," he said. "I like that, Ginger. And it can't have been easy for you. I would have found out in the end, you know."

We started back into the house. Just as I breathed a sigh of relief, my father said, "You do realize you're grounded, don't you?"

"For how long?" I asked, trying to look pathetic.

"Till the end of the month. No parties, no football games, no nothing."

I swallowed hard. "I guess that's fair," I said.

"And you have to make me waffles for breakfast, too," he said.

All in all, things could have been a lot worse. I'd have to miss a few fun things with my friends, but that was a small price to pay for what I had done. And Spirit Rock would still be there to help me through the hard times. And Ben would come to visit and bring me candy bars . . . I started to grin as I made the waffles.

About the Author

Janet Quin-Harkin has written over fifty books for teenagers, including the best-seller *Ten-Boy Summer.* She is the author of the *Friends* series, the *Heartbreak Café* series, and the *Senior Year* series. She has also written several romances.

Ms. Quin-Harkin lives with her husband in San Rafael, California. She has four children. In addition to writing books, she teaches creative writing at a nearby college.

Here's a sneak preview of The Boyfriend Club™ #6:
Roni's Two-Boy Trouble

Drew and I drove home from Cammy Parker's house in silence. There were a lot of things that I wanted to say, but I didn't know how to say any of them. I was scared to ask Drew about Cammy, because I didn't think I'd like his answer.

"Cammy's quite a girl," Drew said at last. "Did you know she got all those trophies in her house for swimming?"

"Well, isn't that nice?" I said sweetly.

He glanced across at me and didn't say anything for a while. Finally he asked, "Do you think your parents will let you come on the trail ride next weekend?"

There was something strange about his tone of voice. It almost sounded like he hoped they wouldn't let me go. And now that I thought about it, I wasn't sure I wanted to go, even if I could afford it. I could just imagine what it would be like—Cammy flirting with Drew, and Drew flirting right back, while everybody else just felt sorry for me.

Suddenly I made up my mind. I wasn't going to be dumped by anyone, not even Drew Howard. If there was any dumping going on, I would be the dumper, not the dumpee!

"Gee, I don't know about next weekend," I said. "I already made plans."

"Oh," he said. I couldn't tell if he sounded relieved or surprised. "Um, okay."

We drove on in silence. "Roni," Drew said at last, "I've been thinking . . . about us. I was wondering whether we should see other people. Not date each other exclusively, I mean. We are kind of young to be tied down, you know. We should be experiencing life—dating different people—so that we make the right choices later on . . . don't you agree?"

He looked at me nervously, as if he was expecting me to burst into tears and beg him to stay with me. That proved he didn't know me very well!

"I think you're absolutely right, Drew," I said breezily. "In fact, I've been feeling the same way myself."

"You have?"

"That's right. I mean, there's plenty of time for

going steady when we're older." I took a deep breath. "I'm so glad you brought this up now, Drew. I've been wondering how to tell you . . . you see, I've been invited on this great date next weekend and . . . and I really wanted to go, but I didn't want to hurt your feelings."

I was incredibly proud of myself. Talk about Oscar-winning performances! Drew was staring at me, dumbfounded. "Date? What date? With who?" he asked sharply.

"Nobody you'd know. This friend of a friend is coming in from New York. He's supposed to be a great guy, and they have this fun weekend planned. And you'll be away on your trail ride, so everything works out perfectly, right?"

"Yeah, I guess it does," answered Drew, but he didn't sound really sure. "Nobody I'd know, huh?"

"Right. But I'm sure he's a fun guy. I bet we'll have a blast."

"Great," he said without enthusiasm.

We didn't say anything else, but I saw him look across at me a couple of times. Finally he pulled up outside my house.

"Well, um, I'll see you around at school, Roni," he said.

"Yeah, see you around, Drew. Thanks for the ride."

I walked into the house with this phony smile on my face. I got all the way to my room and locked the door before I flung myself down on the bed and cried. I couldn't believe I had lost him. I had meant to put up a fight, I had meant to keep him away from Cammy, but obviously I didn't know how.

"Drew," I whispered. He was the best, the most amazing thing that had ever happened to me. I had been shocked when he started to like me in the first place. I suppose I had always known it was too good to last.

Only after my sobs had died down to occasional hiccups did I realize what I had done. I had told Drew that I was going to spend the weekend with another guy. But I hadn't told him the other guy was a nerd. I sat up and stared at myself in my vanity mirror. I wasn't a pretty sight—eyes all red, cheeks blotchy, and hair one big mess. Even a nerd might have run the other way if he saw me like this!

"You can't be serious," I said to myself. I hadn't really meant it when I told Drew about the weekend. I had just said that to make him jealous. Even I wasn't crazy enough to spend a whole weekend with a nerd, was I?

Then I began to think about it. Owen had said his friend Chris would pay well. I really needed spending money—and new outfits—if I was ever going to get Drew back from Cammy. The nerd's friend from New York might not be too bad . . . and it wasn't as if I'd really have to date the nerd. It would just be acting.

And as I had proved today, I was some actress.

The idea didn't sound so crazy anymore. I'd make money, which I desperately needed. If Drew happened to call my house to check on me, my mother could truthfully say that I was out with a couple of guys. If the nerd wasn't too repulsive, it could be done. I didn't think I could handle a weekend with Owen or Ronald, but not all nerds were as annoying as they were. As long as he didn't spill egg down his sweater like Wolfgang or wear taped-up glasses like Walter, it would be okay. I'd just have to make sure we went to a place that no popular kids ever went to. I could never let Drew find out about my date with a nerd.

Boyfriend Club Central asked:

What can you do to cheer up a friend when she's having boy trouble?

And you said:

Offer to let her borrow your favorite sweater.

- Grace L., Syracuse, NY

Make a tape of her favorite songs.

- Donna S., Bakersfield, CA

Call her on the phone and see if she wants to talk about it.

- Melissa L., Margate, NJ

Tell her one of your boy-trouble stories with a happy ending.

- Jennifer B., Seattle, WA

Buy her a funny card.

- Wendy K., North Platte, NE

Try to fix her up with someone else.

- Samantha F., Atlanta, GA

Bring an extra snack in your lunch and share it with her.

- Joanne A., Boston, MA

Now we want to know:

What's the best way to meet a boy you like?

Write and tell us what you think, and you may see your advice in a future ADVICE EXCHANGE:

Boyfriend Club Central
Dept. B
Troll Associates
100 Corporate Drive
Mahwah, NJ 07430